P9-BBP-373

Hi, I'm JIMMY!

Like me, you probably noticed the world is run by adults.
But ask yourself: Who would do the best job
of making books that *kids* will love?
Yeah. **Kids!**

So that's how the idea of JIMMY books came to life.
We want every JIMMY book to be so good that when you're finished,
you'll say,

"PLEASE GIVE ME ANOTHER BOOK!"

Give this one a try and see if you agree.
(If not, you're probably an adult!)

JIMMY PATTERSON BOOKS
FOR YOUNG READERS

James Patterson Presents
How to Be a Supervillain by Michael Fry
Sci-Fi Junior High by John Martin and Scott Seegert

The Middle School Series by James Patterson
Middle School: The Worst Years of My Life
Middle School: Get Me Out of Here!
Middle School: Big Fat Liar
Middle School: How I Survived Bullies, Broccoli, and Snake Hill
Middle School: Ultimate Showdown
Middle School: Save Rafe!
Middle School: Just My Rotten Luck
Middle School: Dog's Best Friend
Middle School: Escape to Australia

The I Funny Series by James Patterson
I Funny
I Even Funnier
I Totally Funniest
I Funny TV
I Funny: School of Laughs

The Treasure Hunters Series by James Patterson
Treasure Hunters
Treasure Hunters: Danger Down the Nile
Treasure Hunters: Secret of the Forbidden City
Treasure Hunters: Peril at the Top of the World
Treasure Hunters: Quest for the City of Gold

For exclusives, trailers, and other information,
visit jimmypatterson.org.

HOW TO BE A
SUPERVILLAIN

Michael Fry

JIMMY Patterson Books

LITTLE, BROWN AND COMPANY
New York Boston London

The characters and events in this book are fictitious. Any similarity to real persons, living or dead, is coincidental and not intended by the author.

Copyright © 2017 by Michael Fry

Hachette Book Group supports the right to free expression and the value of copyright. The purpose of copyright is to encourage writers and artists to produce the creative works that enrich our culture.

The scanning, uploading, and distribution of this book without permission is a theft of the author's intellectual property. If you would like permission to use material from the book (other than for review purposes), please contact permissions@hbgusa.com. Thank you for your support of the author's rights.

JIMMY Patterson Books / Little, Brown and Company
Hachette Book Group
1290 Avenue of the Americas, New York, NY 10104
JimmyPatterson.org

First Edition: May 2017

JIMMY Patterson Books is an imprint of Little, Brown and Company, a division of Hachette Book Group, Inc. The Little, Brown name and logo are trademarks of Hachette Book Group, Inc. The JIMMY Patterson name and logo are trademarks of JBP Business, LLC.

The publisher is not responsible for websites (or their content) that are not owned by the publisher.

The Hachette Speakers Bureau provides a wide range of authors for speaking events. To find out more, go to hachettespeakersbureau.com or call (866) 376-6591.

Library of Congress Cataloging-in-Publication Data
Names: Fry, Michael, 1959– author, illustrator.
Title: How to be a supervillain / Michael Fry.
Description: First edition. | New York : Little, Brown and Company, 2017. | "JIMMY Patterson Books." | Summary: "Twelve-year-old Victor Spoil comes from a long line of famous supervillains and he's fully expected to join their ranks one day. But to his family's utter disappointment, Victor doesn't have a single bad-guy bone in his body. He won't run with scissors, he always finishes his peas, and he can't stand to be messy. Hopeless!"— Provided by publisher.
Identifiers: LCCN 2017003441 | ISBN 9780316318693 (hardback)
Subjects: | CYAC: Supervillains--Fiction. | Superheroes--Fiction. | Identity--Fiction. | Humorous stories. | BISAC: JUVENILE FICTION / Action & Adventure / General. | JUVENILE FICTION / Family / Parents. | JUVENILE FICTION / Science Fiction.
Classification: LCC PZ7.F9234 Ho 2017 | DDC [Fic]--dc23 LC record available at https://lccn.loc.gov/2017003441

10 9 8 7 6 5 4 3 2 1

LSC-C

Printed in the United States of America

To Bill

FOREWORD

When I first read Mike Fry's story about a kid who really, really wants to be good even though his parents really, really want him to be bad, I couldn't help but laugh out loud. We've all gotten scolded by our parents (yes, even someone as ancient as I am was a kid once upon a time) but usually for the exact opposite reason!

You might not think you have much in common with Victor, who's going to grow up to be a supervillain and do battle with superheroes one day, but you'd be surprised. We all have a little bit of good and a little bit of bad in us...and it's up to us to decide which part wins!

Enjoy!

—James Patterson

HOW TO BE A SUPERVILLAIN

My parents used to fight a lot.

Wait. No. Not with each other. They used to fight other people for a living.

Yup. My parents are supers. Supervillains, to be exact. Meet Rupert and Olivia Spoil, otherwise known as...

I know. Pretty lame. But it works for them. Not so much for me.

Let me explain. My name is Victor Spoil. I'm twelve years old and I was raised to be bad.

Which is a problem...

...when you're actually good.

CHAPTER 1

Look at me.

More than lame.

I mean, I try to be bad. Seriously, I do. But it's harder than it looks.

Being bad requires a lack of imagination. You can't allow yourself to imagine what might happen if you do a bad thing.

You have to not care.

You have to not care that your space plane takes up three parking spots. You have to not care that no one appreciates having their car crushed by the overpass that collapses after your Disintegrator Ray misfires. You have to not care that evildoing is very messy and those grass stains on your supersuit are really hard to get out.

I can't do that.

I can't *not* care.

I've tried. Really, I have. I tried running with scissors.

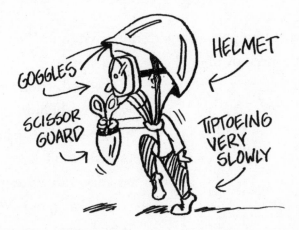

GOGGLES

HELMET

SCISSOR GUARD

TIPTOEING VERY SLOWLY

But I'm not the most coordinated kid and I just hate to make a mess.

I tried not eating all my peas.

But I like peas. They're full of vitamin K *and* a good source of fiber.

I even tried not washing behind my ears once, but it just felt...I don't know... so very, *very* wrong.

I'm a good kid. Which, in my parents' eyes, means I'm a bad kid. But I'm not the *good* kind of bad kid. I'm the *bad* kind of good kid.

My parents try to understand. But it's hard.

It's hard on all of us.

CHAPTER 2

I come from a long line of supervillains.

THE SPOIL FAMILY TREE

ME
VICTOR SPOIL

MOM

DAD

RUPERT SPOIL | THE SPOIL SPORTS | OLIVIA SPOIL

GRANDPA SPOIL   GRANDMA SPOIL   GRANDPA RUIN   GRANDMA RUIN

DR. BUZZKILL   GNAT GIRL   MR. IRRITABLE   MADGE THE HORRIBLE

GREAT-GRANDPA SPOIL   GREAT-GRANDMA SPOIL   GREAT-GRANDPA WHINER   GREAT-GRANDMA WHINER

THE ERASER   MRS. MOPE   SIR SPLEEN   SQUID WOMAN

GREAT-GRANDPA RUIN   GREAT-GRANDMA RUIN   GREAT-GRANDPA HAVOK   GREAT-GRANDMA HAVOK

THE DRIZZLER   LADY SPATULA   SKILLETHEAD   DORIS*
*NOT A SUPERVILLAIN

My parents are minor supervillains and pretty much semiretired. Let's call them supervillain*ish*. These days they're more into battling to take over the recliner than trying to take over the world.

Still, they want what all supervillain parents want. They want me to grow up evil, with a chip on my shoulder and a burning desire to spread chaos and mayhem across the universe.

Did I mention how much I don't like to make a mess?

So instead of a hard-charging destroyer of worlds, they got me: Tidy Boy.

Destroyer of spots.

I feel bad for Mom and Dad. Like I said, I've tried to be bad. And they've tried *everything* to help me be bad. They've tried talking to me....

They've tried punishing me....

They've tried tutors....

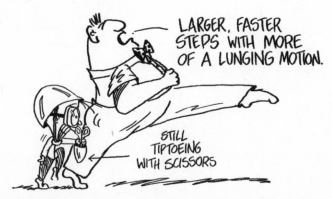

But nothing works. No matter what they do, they can't jump-start the bad in me. I feel bad that I can't be...you know...*bad*.

I especially felt bad that I couldn't be bad after Mom and Dad had the Talk with me.

No, not *that* Talk. The *other* Talk.

The one about how the superworld really works.

CHAPTER 3

It's true. All those crazy battles between supers over, in, and through major cities are staged. They have been for years.

A LONG TIME AGO SUPER-HEROES AND SUPERVILLAINS USED TO FIGHT WITHOUT ANY THOUGHT TO CONSEQUENCES...

BUS

ZAP!

CONSEQUENCES LIKE MAKING SUPERMESSES THEY DIDN'T HAVE TO CLEAN UP.

ONE TIME, AFTER A NASTY BATTLE IN BOSTON, IT BECAME CLEAR THAT ANY SORT OF SUPERFUTURE WAS IN JEOPARDY.

YOU SEE, HEROES AND VILLAINS ARE LOADS OF FUN RIGHT UP UNTIL THE POINT WHERE THE BUS FALLS ON YOU.

FALLING BUS

THE SUPERS HAD A LOT TO LOSE IF THE CIVILIANS TURNED ON THEM. STUFF LIKE FREE COSTUMES, SECRET LAIR SECURITY, ADULATION, AND MOST IMPORTANTLY AWE.

AWE? I LIKE AWE.

AND PIE.

A SUPER THAT DOESN'T BASK IN AWE JUST ISN'T SUPER, HE'S...

JUST LIKE EVERYONE ELSE?

EWWW...

SO THE HEROES AND VILLAINS MADE A TRUCE. NO MORE RANDOM BATTLES. ALL FIGHTS WOULD BE SCRIPTED AND STAGED. JUST LIKE PRO WRESTLING.

FADE IN: EXT. BANK BUILDING

THEY ALSO AGREED TO BE GOVERNED BY THE AUTHORITY. THE AUTHORITY MAINTAINS THE TRUCE. WHOEVER BREAKS THE TRUCE IS SUBJECT TO BEING PURGED.

STRAPPED TO ROCKET

AHHHHHHHH!!

SENT INTO SPACE

SO THE BIG GUNS BATTLED IN THE BIG CITIES WHILE THE MINOR SUPERS WORKED THE SMALL TOWNS.

AS FAR AS THE CIVILIANS KNEW, EVERYTHING WAS AS IT ALWAYS WAS EXCEPT IT STOPPED RAINING BUSES.

... AT THE DES MOINES I-80 OVERPASS, MR. BEAVER VS. THE SPOIL SPORTS!

SUNDAY! SUNDAY! SUNDAY!

HEY! NO BUSES.

IT'S ALL FOR THE BEST, I SUPPOSE. EVERYONE'S HAPPY. IT'S A WIN-WIN, EXCEPT... NO ONE EVER REALLY WINS. AND WE GET TO KEEP THE FREE COSTUMES.

SO THERE'S THAT.

CHAPTER 4

So if it's all just fake, you'd think I should be able to fake being bad. Right?

Wrong. Even after I knew the supertruth, I still couldn't bring on the superbad.

My parents were so disappointed. *Seriously* disappointed. Who-switched-our-child-with-this-goody-goody-at-birth-we-should-change-his-name-to-Disappointing disappointed.

Mom sighed. "What are we going to do with him?"

Dad said, "I have a plan."

"Wait," said Mom. "You don't mean—"

"Mean what?" I asked.

Dad said, "Now that Victor's out of school for the summer, *he* can take him on as an apprentice."

I was confused. "Who can take me on?"

·"Seriously," said Mom. "*He's* the only option?"

"The Walrus turned us down. Mr. Sour Cheeks said no. Even Infectious said, 'Are you kidding?' He's our last hope. And he should be here any second."

Now I was getting anxious. "*Who's* my last hope?"

Dad opened the door and in stepped the lamest supervillain of all time.

He smiled. "The Smear...

I did mention how much I hate messes, didn't I?

CHAPTER 5

The Smear? Not the Smear! Anyone but the Smear!

Why? Because he's...

THE SMEAR!

THINGS THAT MAKE MY UNDERWEAR RIDE UP
(IN ORDER OF INTENSITY)

1. MESSES
2. BEARS
3. MESSY BEARS
4. MESSY LAME SUPERVILLAINS!

There are many supervillains. Hundreds of them. Some of them are pretty cool.

DR. DEPLORABLE PROFESSOR ENIGMA LAVA LADY

Some are okay.

BLOW HARD TWISTER SISTER THE SPOIL SPORTS

A few are seriously lame.

THE
YEASTMASTER

IRON
DUDE

MOLDY
DAVE

And one of them is just pathetic.

Here's how pathetic the Smear is: He once brought a jar of grape jelly to a photon saber fight.

Who brings a jar of grape jelly to a photon saber fight? That's right.

This guy:

Just pathetic.

CHAPTER 6

Dad smiled at the Smear. "This is our son, Victor Spoil."

I backed away. "No way."

The Smear stared. "Well, at least he has a bad attitude."

"You don't understand," I said. "There's no way I'm going to apprentice for you."

Mom applauded. "How rude!"

"Seriously! I'm not going with him," I cried.

The Smear looked at my dad. "I'm not giving back your deposit."

Dad looked at me. Shook his head and sighed. "You want to be a civilian? You want to be like Benny?"

Benny is my uncle. He's the white sheep of the family.

"He makes socks," said Dad. "For a living. Socks. All day. Every day. Socks."

BENNY

SOCKS

BOUTS OF QUIET SOBBING NOT SHOWN

The Smear said, "Look, kid, being a civilian's not so bad. You keep your head down. Get a job. Not socks. That's just...wrong. But I hear they're always looking for janitorial help. Stain cleaner-uppers. Really nasty smear stains with worm guts and lizard brains. You know, the ones that never wash out."

He smiled. "You want to be a stain cleaner-upper? Or a stain thrower-atter?"

Hmm. I had to think about that.

Supervillainish or ordinaryish?
Being bad?
Or being boring?

CHAPTER 7

I looked at Mom and Dad. Then I looked at the Smear. Then at my shoes. They were tied. They're always tied. But the loops were uneven. It bothers me when the loops are uneven. How'd they get uneven? Not sure why. Where was I? Oh, right. No big deal. Just the...

"He's got that look," said Mom.

"What look?" said Dad.

Mom said, "The look he gets at the mall when he has to choose between boxers or briefs."

See, briefs are nice and snug, but boxers don't look so underweary. It's not an easy decision.

"Maybe this was a bad idea," said the Smear.

"NO!" yelled Mom and Dad.

"He's fine," said Mom. "Victor, you're fine, right?"

No, I was not fine. I was faced with an impossible choice. When faced with an impossible choice, I get all panicky, and woozy, and wobbly....

KA-CHUNK

WHOOSH

And fainty.

Mom said, "Oh, my. Maybe he really isn't ready for this."

She knelt down and curved her arms out awkwardly. Like she was hugging the air. Not me. The air. There's not a lot of touching in my family. Touching leads to hugging. And hugging leads to caring. And caring leads to a visit from the Supervillain Police.

Mom said, "Just give it a week, and if you really hate it, you can come home and we'll figure out something else."

Despite the rare display of almost affection, I was still undecided.

The Smear said, "Kid, you ever wonder why I'm the lamest supervillain?"

"Other than the grape jelly?" I said.

I STAINED DR. DEPLORABLE.

WHOA.

"Dr. Deplorable?" I said. "He's the—"

The Smear closed his eyes. "Most evil supervillain on the planet. We used to be partners. Until... the incident."

Dad and Mom took a step back.

Dad pointed at the Smear. "It was YOU!"

"Yeah, yeah, it was me," said the Smear.

"How awful," said Mom.

I shook my head. "What? What?"

Mom went to the bookcase and pulled out an old copy of *Villainy Fair*. She thumbed through the magazine, stopped on a page, and showed me a picture.

"Wait," I said. "Is that a wiener dog on his forehead?"

The Smear just smiled.

I stared at the picture. Then I stared at the Smear. Okay, sure, Mr. Sloppy-Pants here was super lame. But...staining Dr. Deplorable was pretty awesome. And funny. Maybe I could learn a thing or two from this guy. And have some fun.

I like fun.

And pie.

But mostly fun.

CHAPTER 8

"Dr. Deplorable and I worked together on a few battles against Mr. Awesome," said the Smear. "This was before the Truce. Before all the super stuff became super fake."

I was impressed. "Mr. Awesome is the greatest superhero on the planet."

"I heard he has calf implants," said Mom.

"Almost got him in Boston. Over the Common," said the Smear.

Dad said, "The Bostocalypse,

CALF IMPLANTS

from twenty years ago? That's the final battle that led to the Truce."

"The last true fight," said the Smear. "Dr. Deplorable had Mr. Awesome cornered. I went in to blind him with a stain grenade...but it blew up in my hand."

AND DR. DEPLORABLE'S FACE.

KER-SPLAT!

I nodded. "So that's where he got the wiener dog stain."

The Smear sighed. "We lost the battle, and I lost everything when Dr. Deplorable brought me up on charges in front of the DSV. They found me guilty and banished me from superbattling for twenty years."

"The DSV?" I asked.

"Department of Supervillains," said Dad.

"You know, with the administrative office under the volcano?" said Mom. "With endless lines to take a number to get in more endless lines?"

"Back up. They banished you? But the stain was an accident," I said.

"Dr. Deplorable didn't see it that way. That wiener dog never washed out."

"Wow," I said. "Sure, that's not the best look for him, but banned for twenty years!"

The Smear said, "But the twenty years are up, and now I can make a comeback."

"A comeback? Why now?" I asked.

"It's true the battles are fake and the outcomes don't matter," said the Smear. "But I miss the action. There's nothing quite like the thrill of scrawling all over a superhero with permanent marker."

That did sound like fun. As long you wore proper protective gear and didn't scrawl on yourself.

The Smear continued, "I'm set to battle Mega-Mole in Des Moines in three days."

"You remember that time we dangled Mega-Mole over a shark tank in Topeka?" said Mom.

Dad nodded. "Good times."

The Smear laid his hand on my shoulder. Not around my shoulder. Actually *on* my shoulder. It felt weird. But warm.

"It won't be easy," said the Smear. "It won't be glamorous. And it *will* get messy. I can't guarantee fame and fortune. But I can guarantee adventure. And pie."

I lit up. "Pie?"

"Where do you think I get the base for all my smear stains?"

I said, "I like pie."

The Smear lifted his hand off my shoulder, leaving a hand-print stain. Normally, I'd freak out at something like that, but this time was different. This wasn't a stain. This was a mark. A mark of distinction.

The mark of a supervillain's apprentice.

CHAPTER 9

"Have we talked about your evil laugh?" asked Mom the next day as she folded and packed my underwear (boxer briefs).

EVIL LAUGH?

Dad said, "You know, when the supervillain has the superhero cornered, and he or she starts laughing."

"Not because anything's funny," added Mom. "But because it's super creepy. The creepier the better."

I nodded. "Creepy."

"But not too long. You go on too long and the hero can escape," said Mom.

Dad agreed. "Somehow they always squirrel out of it. And they claim *we're* sneaky."

"Wait," I said. "I thought all this was scripted."

"Well, yes and no," said Dad.

Mom said, "There's always a little wiggle room to, um..."

"Improvise," said Dad.

I shook my head. "Improvise?"

Mom and Dad shared a look.

"Supervillains have it tough," said Mom.

Dad closed his eyes. "Brutal."

"Mostly because we lose all the time," said Mom. "It stresses a villain out. All this losing."

Dad nodded. "The therapists we've seen."

"That's why when you have a chance to purple a nurple, you go for it," explained Mom.

Dad turned to Mom. "You remember that time you gave Mr. Platypus a wedgie?"

"It took them almost twenty minutes to pull his underwear out," laughed Mom.

Dad smiled. "Good times."

I said, "So what you're saying is that I should break the rules?"

Mom shook her head. "Victor, rules are made to be broken. By supervillains! It's the law!"

She turned to Dad. "Is he really ready for this? It's a bright, accepting world out there. A young villain could lose his way," said Mom.

Dad looked at me. "He won't lose his way. Will you, son?"

Mom stuck out her lower lip. "But he's my little baby, and I just want the worst from him."

Then—

We all went to the window. It was the Smear. In his Smearmobile.

"I'm going to Des Moines in that?" I cried.

"See, he's not ready," said Mom. "He still cares too much. How can we let him go? We don't know what we'll get back. Remember Mr. Sulfur's son? He came back a *librarian!*"

Dad raised his hand. "We have to let him try."

Mom looked at me. "You really, *really* want to do this?"

I said, "I think so."

Mom looked at Dad and pointed at me. "He *thinks* so."

"It's time," said Dad.

Mom cried, "A LIBRARIAN!"

"It's time," repeated Dad.

I grabbed my suitcase and we all headed downstairs. Part of me was screaming, *NO!* But other parts of me kept walking.

I wasn't sure this was what I wanted to do. But I wasn't sure it wasn't. I knew what would happen if I didn't go. Mom and Dad would be disappointed. And I'd be disappointed that they were disappointed. But if I did go? What then?

That's when I remembered something Grandpa Spoil once said: "You miss one hundred percent of the eye gouges you never gouge."

So I kept walking out the door and toward the Smear. Walking toward what *could* happen. And walking away from what *would* happen.

"Hey, kid," said the Smear. "Ready to kick some MegaMole butt?"

"I guess," I said.

Mom turned to Dad. "He guesses."

Dad insisted, "It's time."

While the Smear threw my bag in the back, Mom cradled the air above my shoulders. "I only want to hear bad things. You understand? Make your mom proud."

Dad shook my hand. "Make us both proud."

I swallowed hard. "Yes, sir."

Mom closed her eyes and shook her head. "He called you 'sir.' We're doomed."

We said our good-byes. I got in the car. The Smear put it in gear, gave it some gas, and...nothing happened.

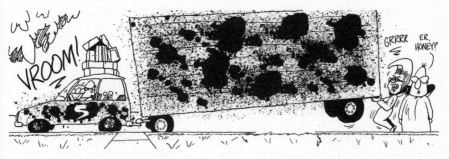

Dad made Mom put the trailer down, then whispered, "It's time."

CHAPTER 10

We weren't halfway down the block before the Smear started my supervillain education. "Pay attention, kid. There's a lot to learn."

I reached into my backpack and pulled out a notebook and pen.

"What are you doing?" said the Smear.

"Taking notes."

The Smear grabbed my notebook and threw it out the window. "First lesson: Supervillains NEVER take notes!"

"How will I remember anything?" I asked.

"You pay attention! With a fierce, burning passion to do evil."

"We'll work on it," said the Smear. "First, let's talk stains."

He started by describing various custom smear stains and their effect on superheroes.

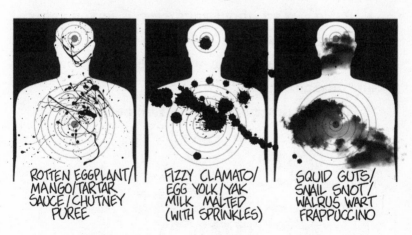

ROTTEN EGGPLANT/ MANGO/TARTAR SAUCE/CHUTNEY PUREE

FIZZY CLAMATO/ EGG YOLK/YAK MILK MALTED (WITH SPRINKLES)

SQUID GUTS/ SNAIL SNOT/ WALRUS WART FRAPPUCCINO

"Can you pick up walrus warts at Costco?" I wondered out loud.

"A little less talking and a little more listening," he said.

Then he turned to his patented stain delivery systems, including but not limited to Stain Soakers....

I said, "What about your eyes? Can you spray stains with your eyes?"

"No," he said. "That would be weird. And really unsanitary."

Then he described a Stain Bomber.

BUCKET O' BLUEBERRY SALSA

"Yum. I'll have some blueberry salsa," I said.

He shook his head. "No. We don't eat the ammo."

"Got it," I said.

Next up was the Stain Mixer....

BAD QUESO DIP

"Wouldn't a flying dump truck be more efficient?" I asked.

He said, "Where's your sense of style? Anyone can make a flying dump truck."

Finally, he described a platoon of specialized, highly trained stain-throwing mice.

"Trained mice?" I asked.

The Smear gestured to the backseat.

I turned back around and stared at the road ahead. "This is going to get strange, isn't it?"

The Smear chuckled. "You have no idea."

CHAPTER 11

We continued down the road while the mice played solitaire in the backseat. I was beginning to feel more comfortable. Maybe this wouldn't be so bad. Maybe this really would be fun.

Meanwhile, the Smear turned on super talk radio.

"Mr. Awesome's on fire! No one's going to stop him!" barked one of the hosts.

"What about Dr. Deplorable?" asked another host.

The first guy said, "Dr. D. is old news. I mean, how do you take him seriously with a wiener dog tattooed on his forehead?"

The Smear smirked. "I did that."

"Hey, check this out," said the first host. "The

Smear and MegaMole are battling in Des Moines this week."

"The Smear?" said the second guy. "I thought he was dead."

"I'm not dead!" protested the Smear.

The first guy said, "No. You're thinking of the Squirm. He tripped and fell into his own piranha tank."

"Oh, right. I always get those two confused," said the second guy.

"Confused?" said the Smear. "The Squirm couldn't hit the broad side of a volcano with a whale!"

"Anyway, the Smear is still a major loser. Stains? WOOOO, I'm so afraid."

The Smear clicked off the radio. "Jerks," he grumbled.

"Um, Mr. Smear?" I asked. "I've been wondering?"

The Smear sighed. "Always with the questions."

"I was wondering about the stains. I mean, it's just a stain. How is a stain going to stop a superhero?"

The Smear didn't say anything. He shot me a look. Not a *That's an excellent question* look. More like a *Who just farted?* look. Then he shouted...

"Right. I get that," I said. "But, you know, a stain is not exactly dangerous. Annoying? Sure. Messy? Of course. But taking out a superhero? I don't think so."

The Smear stared at the road ahead. He breathed a deep sigh. Then he spoke very slowly, "My stains...are feared...across seven continents."

"You've fought in Antarctica?"

"Don't interrupt. My stains don't just stain, they stick...they goo...they get in your hair and between your teeth...in your ears, your eyes...

"Everywhere?" I asked.

The Smear nodded. "Everywhere."

"I guess that would be annoying."

"And the worst is yet to come."

"The worst?"

"Batch number 487B. A superstain...

...THAT CAN STAIN A MAN'S SOUL.

My eyes went wide. "Whoa."

"I'm making a batch back at my secret lair. All I need is the secret ingredient."

"Like eye of newt?"

"That's weird, no."

"Spleen of newt?"

"What's wrong with you?"

"Elbow of newt?"

"Stop talking. The secret ingredient is—"

SCREECH

The Smearmobile skidded to a halt.

"What the…?"

The sudden stop sent all the mice from the backseat into the front windshield (so much for seat belts). I had to wipe a few away to see….

The Smear turned to me. "I did not sign up for this."

CHAPTER 12

"We have something for you!" said Mom. "We forgot to give it to you before you left."

I said, "You couldn't have just sent it to me?"

"Oh, no," said Dad. "Not something *this* important."

Mom said, "It's been in the family for generations. It's a very special hat."

"Special?" I said.

"You know how when you come of age, you find out what your superpowers are?"

"If you have the mutated kind, that is," said Dad. "Or you could be like us and have to come up with your own."

"Seriously?" I asked.

"How did you think you find out if you have mutated powers?" asked Dad.

EXTREME BUTT-KICKING*

* WITH SOME LIGHT TICKLING

"I don't know. Radioactive worm bite? Leaky microwave? One of Mom's special smoothies spiked with a superpower secret formula?"

"No!" said Mom. "That's silly!"

"The black hat is how you find out," said Dad. "When that special time comes and you put it on, your superpowers will be revealed."

"Sounds complicated," I said.

"Not at all," said Dad. "It's spooky and mysterious."

"And a little silly," I added under my breath.

Dad tried to smile (which was difficult for him, since he hardly ever uses those muscles). "Besides, every supervillain starts out with a black hat."

"What are you really doing here?" I said. "Are you checking up on me?"

"Oh, no. Of course not," said Mom.

"You know how your mother worries," said Dad. "'Is he getting enough sugar? Is he remembering to forget to floss? Is he staying up late enough?'"

Mom flashed Dad a look. "You were the one who called Anvil Head."

I looked past my parents. Sitting in the middle of the road was a space plane. Standing next to it was our neighbor Anvil Head.

Anvil Head is very generous with his space plane.

"This isn't about the hat, is it? You're spying on me," I said.

"We're not spying, we're just monitoring you from afar," said Mom.

"Spying," I said. I put my foot down (softly). "I'm not a little boy anymore. I'm fine."

Mom turned to Dad. "Look at him. He's *almost* angry!"

Dad tried to smile again. "It's a start."

"Please go away," I pleaded.

Mom frowned. "Please?"

Dad shook his head. "Ruined it."

The Smear walked up and put his arm on my

shoulder. "Mr. and Mrs. Spoil, your son has a lot of potential. I think he's going to make an impressive supervillain someday."

"You do?" asked Mom, Dad, and I all at the same time.

"Yes," the Smear said, nodding. "Your son has already demonstrated the number one attribute for success as a supervillain: a healthy lack of respect for authority."

"My," said Mom.

Mom and Dad stood there for a second, not sure what to say next.

"We should go," said Dad.

"Yes," said Mom. "Of course."

Mom gave me another awkward air hug, while Dad hovered his hand over my shoulder. "All we ask is you do your worst."

They walked off toward Anvil Head's space plane.

When they were out of earshot, the Smear whispered, "Something to remember: You're not always closest to the people you're related to."

We watched my parents board the plane. Anvil Head started up the engine. The plane rocked back on its rear wheels until it pointed directly up to the sky. Then it took off.

Sort of.

CHAPTER 13

We were back on the road. Des Moines was still a day or so away. All I had was my phone and a bunch of questions. First I checked my messages (six from Mom and Dad), then my e-mail (a Nigerian prince invited me to invest money in his ostrich farm), and then I played Zombie Crush until I helped a zombie out of a bear trap and it bit me (I never win at Zombie Crush).

On to the questions.

"So what's the secret ingredient?" I asked.

"What?" asked the Smear.

"For the super soul stain. The secret ingredient."

The Smear paused. Then he looked down at me somberly and said, "Tears of true sorrow."

"Wait. What?"

"Tears of true sorrow."

"You're kidding."

"What?"

"That is *seriously* lame."

The Smear hit the brakes again.

This time the car and trailer jackknifed. Fortunately, there was no traffic. We spun around and came to a halt in a ditch. I immediately checked the mice in the backseat.

The Smear glared at me. "You think it's *lame?*"

"Pretty much," I said.

"You think *all* of this is lame!"

"No. Well, yeah. Some of it is pretty silly."

"Silly?"

"Tears of sorrow? Superstains? Um...you know, you wear a cape."

The Smear turned away and stared at the corn-fields. "It used to be an honor to be a super. We had a calling. We were part of something bigger than ourselves. Back in the day we really were *super.*"

"Before the Truce."

"Before the Truce we fought for honor, glory, and...

"I've always wondered about that. Why take over the world?"

The Smear stared at me for an uncomfortably long time. Then he asked quietly, "Is that a trick question?"

I shook my head.

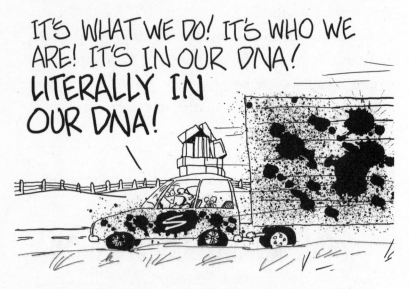

IT'S WHAT WE DO! IT'S WHO WE ARE! IT'S IN OUR DNA! LITERALLY IN OUR DNA!

The Smear's face was beet red. The veins on his forehead pulsed. He looked furious. He looked dangerous. He looked like a super*villain*. A scary, power-mad, soul-staining, evildoing SUPERVIL-LAIN! Suddenly, being his apprentice seemed like a very, *very* bad idea.

I took out my phone and was about to call for help when...

It was an explosion that rocked the Smearmobile like a toy. We were under attack!

"What was THAT?" I yelled.

The Smear yelled, "GET DOWN!"

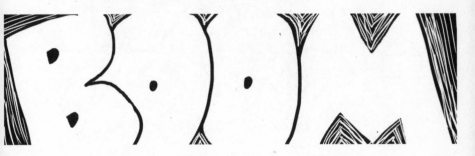

The Smear smiled. "*Someone* doesn't want us to get to Des Moines."

"What? Who? Why? I thought all this was fake!" I yelled as a half dozen mice cowered in my lap.

I turned to look for the Smear, but he was gone. I took stock of the situation. I had myself. I had a cell phone. I was covered with terrified mice. My situation was clear.

Then the strangest thing happened. I looked outside and couldn't believe my eyes. That dumpy, grumpy, middle-aged fake supervillain had suddenly transformed into...

THE SMEAR

On second thought...*sweet* cape.

CHAPTER 14

I'm the son of supervillains. I've seen some stuff. Some posturing. Some scowling. A little finger jabbing. And lots and lots of monologuing.

Monologuing is basically a supervillain's way of saying in fifty-seven words what you could say in three.

YOU THINK WE'RE BAD? YOU THINK WE'RE EVIL? WE'RE JUST LIKE YOU. WE PUT OUR TIGHTS ON TWO LEGS AT A TIME. WAIT. YOU PUT YOUR TIGHTS ON ONE LEG AT A TIME? WHY? TORN TIGHTS? WHERE DO YOU GET YOUR TIGHTS? I KNOW A GUY. I'LL PUT YOU IN TOUCH. NOW, WHERE WAS I?

WE'RE JUST LIKE YOU!

EXCEPT WITH BETTER TIGHTS.

Anyway, I'd seen a lot, but I'd never seen this....

All lameness went out the window. Suddenly
the Smear was...

...pretty darn awesome.

All the firing was coming from a cloud in the sky.

A cloud shaped like a shark!

The Smear commanded the scene. He didn't hesitate. He took action. He was surprisingly limber for a large man.

He was everything I wasn't...

...and wanted to be.

It was over. Whoever, whatever, it was, the Smear won the day.

I freaked out. Superbattles were supposed to be fake. None of what just happened was fake.

I cried, "Those were real explosions! A real shark-cloud space plane! They were really trying to hurt us!"

"Most likely," said the Smear.

"Who was that?!" I yelled.

"No idea," said the Smear.

"But you were yelling at him as though you knew him."

"Standard supervillain patter," he explained. "Pretty common in all situations, whether the opponent is known or not."

Clearly, there was a lot I didn't know about being a supervillain.

The Smear scanned the sky. "I've never seen that type of space plane before. The weapons aren't familiar either. Someone doesn't want us to get to Des Moines. Someone who isn't worried about the Purge."

"Right. My parents told me the Authority uses the Purge as a punishment for the supers. They can catapult you into space if you threaten the Truce."

"You don't die. But you wish you had."

"But so long as we maintain the Truce, we can still have fun, right?"

He took a long look at me. "Fun? Sure. Let's have fun. As long as everybody has fun."

We got into the Smearmobile. I made sure the mice were belted in. The Smear hit the gas. We headed down the road.

I stared at the Smear. Ten minutes ago, I had been ready to bail. But now? I mean, he was amazing. Sure, it had been scary, but somehow the Smear made it less scary. Something changed. Something important. Something weird. It was like there was a fork in the middle of the road, and we took it because...

HEY! FREE FORK!

CHAPTER 16

"MegaMole versus the Smear," chirped Norman as his eyes darted back and forth between the contestants.

We had finally made it to Des Moines and were sitting in a booth at Benny's (Wham Slam Breakfast!) for a prebattle orientation with Norman from the Authority.

Next to MegaMole sat a girl my age. She didn't look too happy to be there. She didn't look too happy to be anywhere.

OCTAVIA

COLONEL KRUNCH

"So, Smear," said MegaMole. "You still headquartered at the Willows of Forestbrook?"

"It's temporary," replied the Smear.

"Wait," I said. "I thought you had a secret lair."

"I do. It's just not as secret as I'd like," said the Smear.

"Seriously? You live in an apartment complex?" I said.

The Smear stared at me. "I said it's temporary, and what did I say about asking too many questions?"

Norman interjected, "Let's talk about why we're here...the battle? Now, MegaMole is the hero. Mr. Smear is the villain. We battle at the railroad yard. Three rounds. All action, including but not limited to punches, kicks, body slams, smear stains, detonations, aerial bombardment, and submarining, will take part within the yard."

I leaned over to the Smear and whispered, "Submarining?"

The Smear pointed at MegaMole. "He likes to dig."

Norman continued, "Any damage to property or civilians comes out of your pay. First round to the Smear. Second round to MegaMole. Third round goes back and forth, with the Smear about to win, only to lose at the last second to Mega-Mole. No punches or stains below the belt. Any questions?"

The Smear raised his hand.

I put my hand out to the girl. "Hi, I'm Victor."

She glared at me. "Am I supposed to be impressed?"

"Octavia!" barked MegaMole. "That's no way for an apprentice hero to behave."

"What. Ever," said Octavia.

MegaMole sighed, "This is Octavia Sparkle, my apprentice."

"Ah, the Sparkles' daughter," said the Smear. "Did that stain on your dad's left elbow ever wash out?"

Octavia glared at the Smear. "No."

The Smear grinned. "Too bad."

"Octavia has a bit of an attitude problem," noted MegaMole.

The Smear looked at me. "Then you two have a lot in common."

A couple walked up and pointed at MegaMole.

The couple looked disappointed. The man said, "Oh, wait. Not the Woodchuck, the Beaver."

"MegaMole!" said MegaMole.

"What's your superpower again?" asked the man.

The Smear smiled. "He likes to dig."

MegaMole glared at the Smear. "Subterranean ambush."

Norman broke in. "Excuse me, but we have business to conduct. I know how fans like to gawk, but supers are people too. They put their tights on one leg at a time just like you."

I raised my hand. "Actually, my parents put their tights on two legs at a time."

"Impressive," said the Smear.

The man smirked. "Freaks. You're all freaks."

Norman stood up. "These gentlemen risk their lives for *your* entertainment. The least you can do is pay them the respect they deserve. Good day, sir!"

The couple turned to leave, but not before the man mumbled, "Freaks in capes."

"I'm sorry you had to hear that, gentlemen," said Norman. "Unfortunately, there's a small portion of the public that is unappreciative of the sacrifices you make to maintain the status quo."

I said, "The Truce."

"Yes," said Norman. "Do I need to remind everyone about the consequences of failing to maintain the Truce?"

MegaMole and the Smear both looked down at their supershoes.

"The Purge," they both said at the same time.

"Yes. *That*," said Norman. "Stick to the script and all will be well."

I looked at the Smear.

Was he listening?

I couldn't tell.

CHAPTER 17

"Is that really what they think we are?" I asked.

The Smear said, "What?"

"Freaks," I said. "Those civilians called us freaks."

"Mostly, yes."

It was evening and we were at the staging area, preparing stains for the next day's battle. It was hot and we didn't want to stain our clothes, so we both stripped down to our underwear.

TINY HIPPOS

PIE

TINY SKULLS

"But we're not freaks," I said. "We're just, you know, *unusual*."

"That's the problem. We have skills and abilities civilians can only dream about. This gives them a choice. They can accept their inferiority, or they can choose to believe we're freaks and therefore somehow less than human."

"But that's prejudiced."

"Yes. Most people are suspicious and fearful of what they don't understand."

"I wonder what kind of powers I'll get?" I asked.

The Smear said, "If it's genetic or mutated, you won't find out till after you come of age."

"When I'm wearing my black hat."

"Right. Yeah, it's weird. I don't make up the rules. Actually, I don't know who made up the rules. Someday I'll figure that out and let you know."

"Thanks," I said.

The Smear continued. "And if you don't get mutated powers, you can be superspecial, like me."

"Superspecial?"

"You get to choose your superskills. Like making superstains, mind writing, electric eel flinging, ooze-spitting snails…anything!"

I was confused. "What if I end up with some lame superpower? You know, like supersmell?"

"You could smell danger," offered the Smear.

"Then what?"

"Not warn others."

"Then what?"

"I don't know. We're all making this up as we go along."

Yes. That. It's all so random and unpredictable. And the unpredictability is the worst part. I'm not good with unpredictability. It makes me nervous. And when I get nervous, I get twitchy. And when I get twitchy, I get sweaty, and when I get sweaty, I get more nervous. It's the Vicious Cycle of Victor. Seriously, it's a thing. They've done studies. Look it up.

The Smear watched me like he knew what I was thinking. "It's all going to be okay."

"How do you know?" I said.

He nodded. "I just do."

CHAPTER 18

Meanwhile, several vats of smear stains bubbled away. The Smear pointed to huge pot on the stove.

BUBBLE BUBBLE

I THINK THE WATERMELON HAS BEEN IN THERE LONG ENOUGH.

I grabbed a pair of tongs and lifted the huge melon. It was covered in a golden-brown crust. It looked like a really fat corn dog.

"What if we explain who we are to civilians?" I asked. "That we're not dangerous, just...you know, different."

The Smear said, "If we're not seen as dangerous, then we're out of a job. No one would care enough to watch our battles."

I carried the deep-fried watermelon to the countertop. "So they love us for being freaks and they hate us for being freaks."

"Civilians—can't live with them, can't enslave them. At least not anymore," said the Smear as he eyed me walking with the watermelon. "Careful now. *That* is a thing of beauty. My best yet. Come to Papa. Come to—"

I started to lift the watermelon onto the countertop, when...

I stared at the mess, afraid to meet the Smear's eye. That thing had been deep-frying for hours. It was too late to start over. I'd screwed up big-time.

I slowly looked up. The Smear wasn't happy.

But then something strange happened. Something I wasn't used to.

The Smear smiled.

"It's okay. Accidents happen," he said. "Are you all right?"

"Yeah. I mean, no. It's just that when I screwed up at home, I mean, I'd get yelled at."

The Smear shook his head. "Not with me, Victor. We're in this together."

That was the first time he'd called me "Victor." Not "kid." And certainly not "Disappointment Boy," like my parents.

Victor.

It felt good.

"Wait," said the Smear. "Before we clean this up, I've got something for you."

He went to one of his storage chests and opened it. He reached inside and pulled out the most wonderful thing I'd ever seen in my whole life.

"Try it on," he said.

CHAPTER *19*

The next morning we arrived at the prebattle meeting, ready to kick MegaMole butt!

While the Smear and MegaMole went over the script with Norman, I started tidying up and organizing the Smear's stain arsenal. I grouped the fruit stains together and separated them from the vegetable-based ones. I stacked the deep-fried stains neatly. I hid the pie-based stains for later. They're super tasty.

I turned around. It was Octavia.

"Where's your costume?" I asked.

"I wouldn't be caught dead in tights and a cape."

I shrugged. "Then why are you here?"

"What do you care?"

"'Cause if I didn't want to be here, I wouldn't be here," I said.

Octavia looked at the ground. "My parents made me."

"Yeah? Mine too. Sort of. It was my decision, but they really wanted me to."

"My parents are all superhero goody-goody and don't understand why I'm not."

"That's weird. My parents are all supervillain evil-evil and wonder why I'm not."

"I'm evil?" asked Octavia.

"In a good way," I said. "I mean, in a bad way. I mean...I don't know what I mean."

"Why are you with a loser like Sir Spills-a-Lot?"

I straightened up (as much as I could in spandex) and glared at her. "He's not a loser. He's a professional failure. There's a difference."

"Victor!" yelled the Smear from across the railroad yard.

"I gotta go," I said.

Octavia rolled her eyes. "Run along to your big, bad, scary master."

"He's not my master. We're in this together. He told me."

"Sure, Stain Boy. Tell yourself that."

The Smear yelled again. "Kid! Get over here!"

I ran to the Smear. He was standing with Mega-Mole, Norman, and two super-old supers I didn't recognize.

"Kid, this is Lasso Girl and the Pollinator. They're our referees."

"So polite. You're sure he's villain material?" asked the Pollinator.

"We're working on it," said the Smear.

"I think he's cute," said Lasso Girl.

The Smear added, "We're working on that, too."

He handed me two water bottles. "Your only job today is to keep these two hydrated."

"Hydrated? But what about the stains and the mice and, you know, watching your back?"

"You gotta crawl before you can walk, kid. Let's start small and work our way up."

This was *not* what I'd signed up for. I'd signed up to learn to be a supervillain. Supervillains wreak havoc. They spread chaos. And look cool doing it. Supervillains do not hydrate.

I looked past the Smear to a sparse crowd in a roped-off area of the railroad yard. Mostly older people, retired, out of work, homeless. One guy looked lost.

"Welcome to the big time," said Octavia behind me.

I turned. She was grinning from ear to ear.

"You're enjoying this," I said.

"Yes. Misery loves company."

"I'm not miserable. I'm just disappointed."

"Get used to it, dude. This whole superracket is on its last legs." She pointed to the Smear and MegaMole. "It's obvious. Obvious to everyone...

...EXCEPT THEM.

TUG TUG

SCRATCH SCRATCH

I wasn't going to admit it out loud, but she was right. All of a sudden this whole thing felt super lame. And I was a super-lame part of it. Good thing no one I knew could see me right now.

"Victor! Yoo-hoo! Over here!" yelled someone who sounded suspiciously like...

CHAPTER 20

"Where's your black hat?" asked Mom.

"I have my own costume now," I said.

Dad said, "But black goes with everything."

"Forget the hat!" I shouted. "What are you doing here?"

They looked confused.

"Miss your superdebut? Not a chance," said Mom. "Though I like the irritation I'm seeing."

Dad said, "Hold on to that. You can never be too irritated."

"I'm irritated because *you're* here," I whispered. "Not because...oh, never mind."

They weren't listening. They never listened. They saw what they wanted to see, and if what they wanted to see was a nasty, mean, rotten kid, who was I to *disappoint* them?

"Oh, my...chills!" whispered Mom.
Dad added, "Almost like he means it."

"Knock 'em dead, son," said Dad. "Well, not dead. We don't do dead anymore. But, you know, knock 'em...um, down."

"Down is good," said Mom.

Like I said, *hopeless.*

"Hey, kid!" yelled the Pollinator. "I'm thirsty."

And with that my great career as a supervillain's apprentice began. Not with a bang, but with a slurp.

I watched the Smear and MegaMole stand at the center of the railroad yard.

The announcer boomed, "Today's match pits the subterranean savior MegaMole versus...wait, who? I thought he was dead. You're sure? If you say so. MegaMole versus the S'more!"

"Smear!" yelled the Smear.

"Sorry. Smear," corrected the announcer.

And we were off to a great start.

As I stood there, water bottles in hand, I realized I was stuck. Stuck between my clueless, pushy stage parents and a tragically lame supervillain sideshow.

What to do? Disappoint Mom and Dad, or stay with Lord Splatterfest and learn the smear stain potential of rotten avocados? Run away and make socks? Or just stand there and do nothing and see what happens?

INDECISIVE BOY

FETAL POSITION →

SUPERPOWERS
1. INDECISION
2. CONFUSION
3. MUMBLING
4. ABILITY TO STAND COMPLETELY STILL
5. FREQUENT FLOSSING

I liked that list. You can't make a wrong decision if you don't make one at all. Indecisive Boy to the rescue!

Lasso Girl walked up. "Water me, sweetheart."

I gave her a bottle. She took a long swig, then looked me hard in the eye. "You know, just because it's all fake doesn't mean it's not real."

"Huh?" I said.

"You'll see."

The battle began and I did see. I saw a lot.
I saw it all.

CHAPTER 21

Round one began.

Sort of.

Superbattles involve a LOT of circling.

Followed by insults...

The referees stopped the battle.

"Whoa, whoa, whoa," shouted the Pollinator.

"That was a cheap shot."

"What?" protested the Smear. "Parentage isn't off-limits."

"Parentage, spouses, kids, aunts, uncles, first cousins are all off-limits," said Lasso Girl.

"Since when?" asked the Smear.

The Pollinator said, "Since the 2016 Amended Supers Agreement. Don't you read our e-mails?"

The Smear shook his head. "What's next? Pets?"

Lasso Girl nodded. "They're under consideration with the Rules Committee."

"This isn't a superbattle, this is a pillow fight," growled the Smear.

"We just want to establish a safe space," said MegaMole.

"This is a superbattle!" cried the Smear. "There's no safety in superbattles!"

"No arguing with the referee," said the Pollinator. "Now get on with it!"

And...they circled some more.

I watched as Norman checked his script. "We circle. We insult. We circle some more. And now...

And boy, did they fight. They fought on the ground.

CLENCH!

UNCLENCH!

They fought from the air.

They fought underground.

They were really fighting. It didn't look fake. It didn't looked staged. It looked *serious*.

It looked awesome!

And I wasn't the only one who thought so. Most of the crowd was really into it. I mean, mostly.

Okay, okay, at least they were awake.

There was one fan who was a bit too into it.

The crowd didn't see two slightly paunchy old men. They saw two superhuman gladiators fighting for glory or world domination or bragging rights at Benny's.

Lasso Girl pointed to the crowd. "You see? It's real to them."

She was right. Sure, I'd been to battles with

my parents. But I guess I wasn't paying attention.
The fans saw *exactly* what they wanted to see.

It made me wonder.

What did *I* want to see?

CHAPTER 22

Round two. The first round had been scripted so that the Smear would have the upper hand. Now it was MegaMole's turn to even the score.

Here's what was supposed to happen....

FADE IN:

The Smear starts well, but MegaMole takes charge and wins the round easily.

FADE OUT.

THE END.

What really happened was...

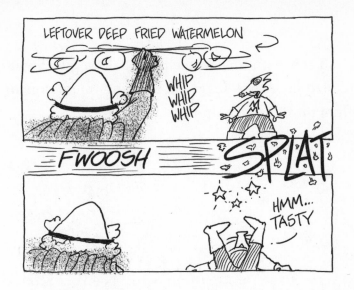

Followed by an aerial strike...er, dump from the flying Stain Mixer.

Then, with MegaMole pinned down, the Smear called in Mouse Team Six to go all trampoline on him until he gave up.

That was when Norman from the Authority started freaking out.

It was only the second round, and MegaMole looked done for. The Smear was smiling. Okay, sure, it'd been twenty years since he fought. And that's a long time to go without a win, but he was scripted to lose this round. He *had* to lose! What had happened to protecting the Truce? What had happened to playing within the rules?

Suddenly MegaMole was gone. One second you could see him struggling under the weight of all those stains and jumping mice. And the next second he disappeared.

UH-OH...

For a few seconds nothing happened, then there was a low rumble that got louder and louder and...

...LOUDER!

MegaMole was tunneling back and forth underneath the Smear. Faster and faster and faster he dug. The ground under the Smear started to boil.

The Smear was slowly sinking into the muck. Within seconds he would be sucked under. There was nothing I or anyone could do. It was all over. And then it wasn't.

BING! BING!
DING! DING! DING! DING! BING!
BING! BING! BING!

The Smear was saved by the bell. MegaMole surfaced. The ground firmed up, so I was able to rush over and pull him out.

"What happened?" I cried.

The Smear grinned. "Pretty cool, huh?"

Norman shrieked, "NO! Not cool! *None* of that was in the script!"

"Hey," said the Smear. "I lost that round like I was supposed to." He wiped himself off and started to walk back to his corner. "So I made a few changes to the script, big deal."

Norman chased after him. "You're not authorized! You don't have clearance. This is not the way this is supposed to work!"

The Smear stopped, grabbed Norman by the throat, and not so gently lifted him to eye level.

The Smear stormed off.

I ran after him. "Um...you're still going to lose the match, right? You're supposed to lose. You have to lose. You don't lose, and the Truce is in jeopardy, and I may never find out what my superpower is! Tell me you're going to lose."

"I'm going to lose."

"Are you just telling me that? Or are you really going to lose?"

STICK AROUND AND FIND OUT.

CHAPTER 23

This was getting out of control. Surely, the Smear wasn't going to risk breaking the Truce just to prove he was the better man in tights.

"What about the Purge?" I asked. "I can't be catapulted into space. Space is cold. Dark. It smells like wet cats. And I'll never find out my superpower!"

The Smear smiled. "Relax. One villain going off script in Des Moines isn't the end of the world. No, it'll take a lot more than that."

The third round started and I had no idea what was going to happen. Neither did Norman.

Apparently, Norman gets chatty when he gets nervous.

The third round dispensed with the circling and the insults and got right to the action. The match was scripted to go to MegaMole, but who knew what the Smear had planned.

Everyone knows that the weakest link to any super is the thumb. Take out the thumb and it's pretty much impossible to be a super. How would you get your tights on?

Lasso Girl and the Pollinator tried to stop the battle. But it was no use. The Smear ignored them. He had MegaMole at his mercy and he wasn't going to let him go.

"You're mine! All mine!" crowed the Smear.

"Stop!" I yelled.

The Smear dropped the whimpering Mega-Mole with a thud. Then he turned and stared right through me. I felt cold. And alone. Again.

"You're supposed to lose," I said. "You *have* to lose."

"No. It's been twenty years. It's time to win. For once. For me. And you."

"But this isn't what I want."

"You don't know what you want," said the Smear as he turned back to the moaning Mega-Mole. "One day you'll understand."

Then he pounced. MegaMole tried to dig his way out, but it was no use. The Smear had him. And if someone didn't stop him, he was going to win the battle.

And break the Truce.

I looked around. Lasso Girl and the Pollinator were backing away. Norman was hiding behind the vegetable stains. The spectators were on their feet, leaning in to watch a fake battle suddenly become very, very real.

Maybe I didn't know what I wanted. But I sure

knew what I didn't want. And that was to have my supervillain career end before it had even started by being Purged into space because some old guy didn't want to be a loser.

"NO!" I screamed as I sprinted toward the Smear.

My momentum bowled him over, setting Mega-Mole free just as the round ended.

Saved by the bell.
Again.

CHAPTER 24

"Why did you do that?" cried the Smear.

"Someone had to stop you," I yelled. "Someone had to save you from yourself."

The Smear looked around. He suddenly seemed to realize what had almost happened. He seemed confused. Like he'd just woken up from a bad dream.

"You?" he asked.

"I'm your apprentice! You said we were in this together!"

"Victor! What did you do?" yelled Mom as she and Dad ran up. "You stopped him!"

Dad shook his head. "Why can't you do the wrong thing? Just once?"

Wrong? I did do the wrong thing. Because it was

the right thing. I think. It's so confusing. I mean,
I saved the Smear from breaking the Truce and
getting us Purged. It was Mom and Dad who were
wrong—or right—about me. Why couldn't they
just let me be wrong—or right—all on my own?

RIGHT ME   WRONG ME

See! You can't even tell the difference!

"This is all my fault," said the Smear calmly. "I
got carried away, and Victor here pulled my butt
out of the fire. I'm sorry, Victor. I apologize."

Mom shook her head. "Supervillains *never*
apologize."

The Smear looked at me. "Well, this one does."

Then he knelt down so we were at eye level,
and said, "Victor, as you're finding out, being a
supervillain isn't easy."

"True that," said Dad.

The Smear continued, "In this fake scripted superuniverse we're supposed to do what we're told. Not what we feel in our hearts is the right thing to do."

"*Wrong* thing," said Mom.

"Not helping," said the Smear.

"You want to win, but you can't win," I said.

The Smear nodded. "Back there I wanted to win. But you stopped me. As you should have. This is why I need an apprentice. An apprentice like you. I need you to stop me from doing something foolish."

I blinked. Then I blinked again. What did he say?

"You need me?" I asked.

"I sure do," said the Smear. And then he did something really weird. He *hugged* me. An actual hug. No air between us!

"Hey," said Mom. "Supervillains don't hug. It's in the rule book. Chapter seven, paragraph fourteen: 'Supervillains should refrain from touching at all times. Unless they're punching, throwing, kicking, or bowling over a superhero. Then it's okay.'"

"I don't like this either," said Dad. "I think we

made a mistake with Mr. Smear here. He was supposed to make you into a real supervillain, not some sort of namby-pamby, softhearted snow-flake. Victor, time to come home!"

I looked at my parents. If I wanted to go back home, now was the time. I could bail. No more worrying about Truces and Purges. No more supervillain apprentice. Just lots and lots of silver-ware to polish. Suddenly my decision was easy. I knew exactly what I needed to do.

"No?" said Dad. "You can't say no. Well, you could if you were a bad kid. But you're not a bad kid. You're a good kid."

"Much to our disappointment," added Mom.

There was that word again. *Disappointment.*

I kept hearing it over and over. I'd had enough. I went full junior supervillain on my parents.

My parents looked seriously confused. Like that time I gave them a pencil holder I'd made at school.

"I think he means it," said Dad.

"I think he does," agreed Mom.

"He stays with me," said the Smear.

I looked up at him. "I'm staying with him."

"But—" said Mom.

"He's made his decision," said Dad.

Mom said, "But he NEVER makes decisions!"

I said, "Say good-bye to Indecisive Boy, say hello to the Decision Kid."

"I think we need to workshop some other names," said the Smear.

"Oh, okay," I said.

"Come, let's go, dear," said Dad.

Mom started to give me another air hug, then stopped. She looked a little sad, though it was hard to tell with the mask.

They walked to the edge of the railroad yard, where Anvil Head's space plane was waiting. Anvil Head waved at me. I waved back. Mom and Dad boarded the plane and took off.

Leaving me with the Smear.

My pal. My buddy.

Someone who needed me.

CHAPTER 25

Now what?

I'd just sent my parents packing, and now I was stuck with a sort of cool, slightly insane, mostly messy...superish-villainish dude.

SPRAY!

Maybe it was too late, but I decided to take inventory and list the pros and cons of my situation.

PROS

1. GLORY
2. SUPERVILLAIN DISCOUNT AT BENNY'S
3. CUTE MICE
4. PIE
5. NO PARENTAL SUPERVISION

CONS

1. CRAZY, BOSS WHO MAY OR MAY NOT WANT TO TEAR APART THE SUPER WORLD

Hmm...not exactly a rousing endorsement.

The bigger problem was what exactly was going on with the Smear. Was it just about winning? Was he trying to bring on the Purge? Or was he just standing up for supervillains everywhere? And what was the deal with that superdude in the shark-cloud space plane who attacked us? Who was he and what did he want? Was he trying to stop the Smear, or did he have some other *secret* agenda?

Why all the secret agendas? Does anyone have an obvious agenda? Like one they could put on a sweatshirt?

Too much uncertainty. Despite the whole Decision Kid thing, I still don't do well with un-certainty. I'm one of those where-are-we-going-when-are-we-going-to-get-there-what's-going-to-happen-when-we-do kind of people.

"Uh-oh," said the Smear.

We were cleaning up after the battle, bottling up the stains, putting away the weapons, feeding the mice (they only eat lasagna, go figure), when the Pollinator and Lasso Girl walked up.

The Smear said, "This can't be good."

They looked upset. But, as it turned out, not with us.

"Against our recommendations," said the Pollinator, "the DSV has decided in its infinite wisdom to promote you to Supervillain First Class."

"It seems your off-script ad-libs proved entertaining to the crowd," added Lasso Girl.

The Pollinator said, "You got over a million views on SuperBattles.com already!"

"A million?" said the Smear.

"Wait," I said. "This whole thing was being shown live online?"

Lasso Girl said, "Of course. All the battles are streamed. Even the minor leagues."

"But no minor-league event has ever gotten this much attention," said the Pollinator.

I checked my Phlitter feed. @TheRealSmear had followers. Not a lot. But it was a start.

"You're blowing up," I cried.

"I like to blow stuff up," said the Smear with a smile.

"The DSV wants you to fight a series of battles

leading up to a rematch with MegaMole," said the Pollinator.

Lasso Girl added, "Battles you will win."

"Oh? Tell me more," said the Smear.

They told us we were going to battle in Omaha, Sioux Falls, and Fargo, then back in Des Moines. Not exactly the big time, but it was a start.

Huh. Sometimes things work out for the best. Maybe worrying about what was going to happen next was a waste of time. Maybe it was about trust. Or faith. Or something.

Whatever it was, I knew one thing: Hanging out with the Smear beat hanging out at home any day.

RING-RING-RING

It was my parents. I didn't answer.
"Who was that?" asked the Smear.
"Nobody," I said.

CHAPTER 26

Before we packed up all the gear and headed to Omaha, I decided to try on my black hat and see if anything fizzed, or sizzled, or rippled, or something.

Oh, well, maybe next time.

The trip to Omaha was uneventful. The mice didn't end up in the front seat once.

A couple of times I thought I saw Anvil Head's space plane following us, but it turned out to be a reflection from the mice's sunglasses in the backseat.

There was a moment there when I was happy my parents might be following. But then I thought, *No, I'm on my own now. I don't need their help. I'm tight with the coolest supervillain of all time.*

Never mind.

After several hours of unfortunate rapping, we finally arrived the next day at an abandoned racetrack in Omaha.

MegaMole and Octavia were there too. We weren't scheduled to fight MegaMole until the rematch. In the meantime we would be fighting other superheroes.

I walked over to Octavia. "Hey," I said.

She stared at the ground. "Hey."

"What's wrong?"

"What isn't wrong?"

"Huh?"

"You and I are sidekicks to the lamest supers in the world."

"Actually, we're not sidekicks," I said. "That would be a step up."

"Not helping," said Octavia as she pointed to the grandstand.

"Your parents?" I asked.

Octavia gave them a halfhearted wave. "How can I miss them if they never go away?"

"You could just tell them to go away."

"Like that'll work."

"It worked for me."

"Wait. Your parents are gone? How?"

"I just said, 'Go away.' But louder. And there may have been some fist shaking."

"And they just left?"

"They weren't happy about it. I think it caught them off guard. I guess they didn't think I had it in me. But since I've been on the road with the Smear, I've changed."

She paused and looked at me like she really wanted to know. "Changed? Changed how?"

"I'm on the verge of being decisive. I got into three arguments yesterday, I absolutely insisted on gluten-free mac 'n' cheese...*and* the old me would never have worn the same pair of socks two days in a row. Now?"

DUDE, YOU'RE OUT OF CONTROL!

"I *know!*" I said.

Octavia looked up at her parents again. "Please leave," she whispered.

"They're hopeless."

"They're parents."

CHAPTER 27

Say hello to the Smear's next opponent:

CATMAN FU

NOT A WORKING TAIL →

HE'S A CAT! AND A MAN! WITH ALL THE FU!

Yeah. That guy.

The Smear told me Mr. Fu's real name is Abner Reynolds. Back in the day he was thinner and hairier, and packed a mean kick. But now?

Not so much.

Meanwhile, great news! No more water-boy duty for this kid. I was promoted to big-boy apprentice. My duties included...

The cheerleading wasn't really necessary, since
the Smear absolutely destroyed Mr. Fu.

The crowd loved it, but Norman from the Authority had a different reaction. He marched up to the Smear and barked, "You were supposed to win, not embarrass the man."

"You're kidding. Look at him," said the Smear. "The embarrassment train left the station a *long* time ago."

The Smear stormed off. I followed and caught up with him.

"What's going on?" I said.

The Smear stopped and turned to me. "I won."

"Yeah, that's good, right?"

"It doesn't feel good. It feels fake."

"Well, it *is* fake."

He said, "I know, but I thought I could pretend it was real. I thought it didn't matter that it was fake. But it does matter. It matters a lot."

I stopped. "It doesn't matter to me."

"What?"

"None of this is about fake battles. It's about showing that supervillains matter. That you can't have a good guy without a bad guy. That supervillains are awesome!"

"You think I'm awesome?"

I nodded.

The Smear's eyes popped. "Whoa."

I continued, "I mean, when you're not yelling at me or feeling sorry for yourself, you're pretty cool."

The Smear stood there for a second. Then he put his hand on my shoulder (AGAIN!) and smiled. "Thanks, kid. You're pretty awesome yourself."

My phone rang. It was my parents again. They wanted to FaceTime.

I didn't answer.

CHAPTER 28

"Hey," said Octavia.

"Hey," I said.

I was packing up the stains. Hosing down the bomber. Herding the mice. Getting ready to leave for the next gig, in Sioux Falls.

Octavia asked, "Can I help?"

"Don't you have stuff to do for MegaMole?"

"Like what? Shave his back?"

"Gross."

"MegaMole is pretty low maintenance. He doesn't really need an apprentice. He's probably just doing it as a favor to my parents."

"They're still around?"

"You want me to tell 'em to get lost?"

"Oh, please, big strong boy. Come to my rescue before I melt into a puddle of spineless goo."

"You're being sarcastic."

"You think? No. I can handle my parents. But there is something you *can* do for me."

"What?" I asked.

"Let's swap places in the rematch," said Octavia. "You apprentice for Squinty, and I'll back up Mr. Smelly-Pants."

"We can't do that. It's against the rules!"

"Who cares about the rules? Just loan me your costume. They'll never know."

"Wait," I said. "You said all this super stuff was lame."

Octavia shrugged. "I did. But at least your guy kicks major butt. He's crazy, but in an insane way. He's *dangerlicious*."

"Is that a thing?"

"It is now. So what do you say?"

IT FEELS WRONG, LIKE A LIE.

"Wait," she said. "Aren't you in training to be a supervillain? As in bad, terrible, untrustworthy, sneaky, and evil?"

She had a point. But then again the Smear wasn't any of those things. Even though he was a supervillain. Sort of.

I was confused.

I said, "I don't know. It seems like—"

Octavia interrupted, "Just think about it."

She took off and I was left wondering. Was I really supervillain material? I liked what the Smear was doing. I liked that he was standing up for villains everywhere. That was a good thing. From a bad guy. So did that make him good? I mean, he had a good heart.

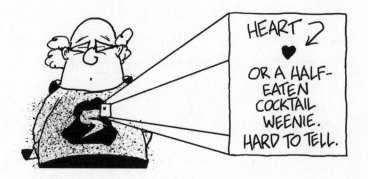

In there. Somewhere.

CHAPTER 29

We arrived in Sioux Falls the next morning and were met by a gaggle of strangely familiar fans.

This was where we met the Smear's number one fan: Alice Dupenski. How did we know she was number one?

HOME-MADE SMEAR ACTION FIGURE

SMEAR TATTOO*

*PERMANENT MARKER

I'M YOU'RE BIGGEST FAN!

UNLICENSED CHINESE KNOCK-OFF SMEAR HOODIE

Pro tip: BEWARE your number one fan.

The Smear was very nice to her. He signed her forehead and posed for a selfie. Then he turned to me and whispered, "Make her go away."

Fortunately, we had plenty of stuff to bribe her with. I gave Alice some hat pins and a stuffed Smear that talked when you squeezed its belly.

THE SMEAR IS HERE!
AND HE DEMANDS ROOT BEER!

SQUEEZE

$19.95 ON AMAZON

She seemed satisfied.

The next match was in a few hours at an abandoned rock quarry. Our next opponent was Professor Tuba.

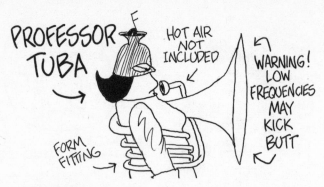

You think I'm making this stuff up. But I'm not.
Professor Tuba used her modified instrument to blast super-low-frequency sound waves that would obliterate anything in their path.

And if that didn't work, she'd just throw the tuba at you.

Again, she didn't seem like too much of a challenge until the Smear told me otherwise.

"She's unpredictable," said the Smear. "She doesn't care about the script any more than I do."

"But you're supposed to win, right?" I said.

"Doesn't matter. I dated her sister years ago. It didn't end well. She's never forgiven me. For her, this is all payback."

The Smear continued, "This'll be the first *real* battle you've seen. I need you to keep down, stay dry, and for God's sake, get out of the way of that sonic sandblaster."

First real battle? I wasn't ready for this. It was one thing when it was all pretend. It was another when there was a real risk of being tuba-blasted to Victoreens.

The battle started in the usual way, with some circling, followed by insults....

And then they got down to business....

Professor Tuba looked done for. There was only one thing she could do....

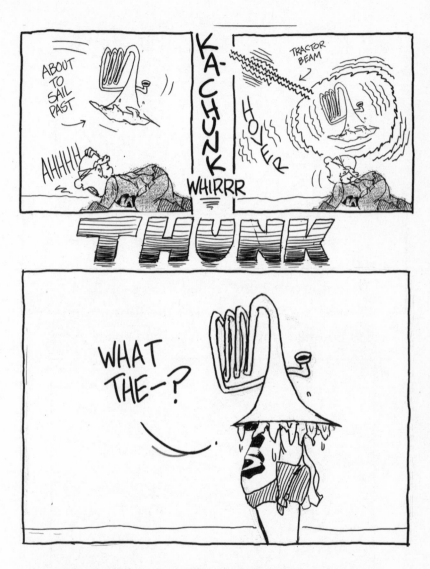

I looked for the source of the tractor beam.

"Again?" cried the Smear as he struggled to get the tuba off his head.

"What is going on?" yelled Professor Tuba.

Just as the Smear removed the tuba, a sinister voice boomed from the shark-cloud space plane.

The Smear looked shocked...and a little afraid.
"I know that phlegm-clotted cough anywhere.
That's...

...DR. DEPLORABLE!!

MY TUBA!

WHOOSH!

BOOM!

CHAPTER 30

Of course Dr. Deplorable would show up in his shark-cloud space plane and use a tractor beam to drop a tuba on the Smear and then blow us all to Victoreens and Smeareens and Tubaeens.

Who didn't see that coming?

WHIP

BOOM!

I DIDN'T SEE THAT COMING!!

As the attacks from above continued, we took cover behind two large rocks. Our only advantage was that we were battling in a quarry filled with boulders to hide behind.

"Why is he shooting at us?" I cried.

The Smear yelled, "He's mostly shooting at me!"

"Okay, so if I run away from you, I'll be safe?" I asked.

"Maybe. Maybe not. Hard to tell with Dr. D.," said the Smear. "He's got a temper problem."

"Did you date his sister too?" Professor Tuba growled from behind a nearby boulder.

"No!" said the Smear. "Remember? We were partners back in the day."

"Then why is he trying to kill you?" I said.

"It's pretty simple, actually," said the Smear.

He continued, "And with me out of the way, he's free to..."

"To what?" I yelled.

The Smear stared at me. "We have to stop him!"

Professor Tuba cried, "With what? Rocks?"

Then suddenly everything began to shake and rattle. The ground started cracking and rising and forming into...*what?*

"Hey, Smear," said two rock monsters.

"ROCK MONSTERS!" I screamed.

"Relax. They're on our side," assured the Smear.

"ROCK MONSTERS!" I screamed again.

"Will you please stop saying that," asked the Smear.

"ROCK MONSTERS!" I screamed a third time.

The Smear stared at me. "Now you're just embarrassing yourself."

Before I could scream "rock monsters" a fourth time, Bob and Dave positioned themselves to take on direct fire from the shark-cloud space plane.

"The blasts are ricocheting back at the shark cloud!" I cheered.

It didn't take long for the space plane to start taking fire. Realizing he couldn't shoot his way out, Dr. Deplorable retreated. But not before issuing a final warning.

And then he was gone.

I said, "He should really have that cough checked out."

The Smear shook his head. "Doctors make the worst patients."

CHAPTER 31

"Tickling?" I said.

The Smear nodded. "Tickling."

"Dr. Deplorable's secret weakness is that he's afraid of being tickled?"

"It's his only weakness. It incapacitates him. And makes him laugh. He really hates to laugh."

I tried to keep a straight face. I failed.

We both laughed. Hard. Like two friends sharing a secret are supposed to laugh.

"And those rock monsters? What's that about?" I asked.

"Aliens," said the Smear. "They missed their ship home. The Authority put them to work providing muscle."

"Their names are Bob and Dave?"

"Their real names can only be pronounced with a mouthful of peanut butter."

We laughed again. How much weirder could things get?

Don't answer that.

"Dr. D. is up to something," said the Smear. "Something that demands me, and now you, out of the way."

"Me?" I said.

"I thought we were in this together," said the Smear.

I smiled. Together. That sounded good. Better than apart. And a lot better than alone.

"Of course," I said.

Norman walked up, followed by the rock monsters.

"This is all highly irregular!" cried Norman. "Dr. Deplorable was not scheduled to participate today. These changes to the script will not be tolerated."

"Maybe you should write a new script," said the Smear.

"And what would it say?" asked Norman.

The Smear smiled. "Stuff happens."

Bob and Dave giggled.

"*Not* funny," said Norman. "Stuff does not happen unless it's properly requisitioned and I approve! Got it?"

"Good luck with that," offered the Smear.

Norman walked off, mumbling to himself.

NO RESPECT. I KILL MYSELF FOR THESE BOZOS IN BOXER BRIEFS! AND THEY MOCK ME! MOCK ME! I SHOULD'VE LISTENED TO MOTHER. I SHOULD'VE STAYED IN SOCKS!

I said, "There must be a lot of money in socks."

"I wouldn't know," said the Smear.

We started to clean up. As we packed for the next gig, I realized something was bugging me. Here we were, fighting fake battles, giving the fans their money's worth, and everyone was mad at us. Dr. Deplorable was up to no good. Norman was beside himself. Professor Tuba was sulking.

WILL SOMEBODY PLEASE TELL ME WHAT JUST HAPPENED!

"Why are we doing this again?" I asked.

"You said I was making a difference," said the Smear. "Standing up for supervillains everywhere."

"Yeah. I guess. It's just that no one seems to appreciate it."

"That just means we're doing it right."

"Huh?"

"Victor, take a seat."

I sat down as the Smear pointed to what was left of the crowd. "You see those fans over there? Their lives are dull, boring, and predictable. No winners. No losers. Just socks. Lots and lots of socks."

THE SMEAR HE IS A DEAR
SO NEVER FEAR
SOMETHING, SOMETHING
ROOT BEER!!

I said, "Alice told me she makes garden gnomes for a living."

"You're missing my point. What I mean is they need us. You were right. They need black and white. Good and evil. Light and dark. Real winners and real losers."

"And we're the losers."

"No. Well, yes, sometimes. But in the grand scheme of things we're mostly winners."

"How so?"

The Smear stood up. "We supers perform a public service by distracting civilians from their dreary lives. It's a noble cause."

"Wait. That makes us sound like good guys."

"Sometimes the bad guys have to act like good

guys so they'll turn out to be better bad guys. Two sides of the same coin."

I was confused. "Huh?"

"We're like a public utility," said the Smear. "Like the electric company. The villains turn the lights off. The heroes try to keep them on."

I knew this one. "And what goes on in the dark..."

The Smear smiled. "Stays in the dark."

"I guess that's why we have to wear black all the time."

"Bad guys *get* to wear black. Good guys *have* to wear white.

BLACK IS MUCH MORE SLIMMING!

CHAPTER 32

Fargo, North Dakota, is a long way from everywhere and everything. Like warmth and decent Mexican food.

The Smear and I were seated at a booth in Fargo's premier Mexican/Chinese restaurant, Taco Gong.

"This is not a chalupa," said the Smear. "This is soggy toast covered in spray cheese."

I said, "Put salsa on it. Salsa makes everything better."

"Because you can't taste anything else."

"Exactly."

"So who are we battling today?" he asked.

The Smear groaned. "I hate that guy."

"I think you're supposed to. You're mortal enemies."

"No, I mean I really hate him. He once shrank himself down, sneaked into my hotel room, and spit on my toothbrush."

"Gross!"

"I know!"

"How are you going to defeat him?"

"What's the script say?"

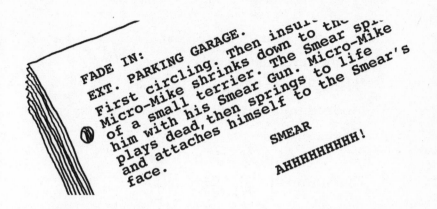

FADE IN:
EXT. PARKING GARAGE.
First circling. Then insult the
Micro-Mike shrinks down to the
of a small terrier. The Smear sp
him with his Smear Gun. Micro-Mike
plays dead, then springs to life
and attaches himself to the Smear's
face.

SMEAR
AHHHHHHHH!

The Smear frowned. "No. No one touches the face."

"I guess we're going off script again," I said nervously.

The Smear smiled. "Relax. Find me a flyswatter and a vacuum cleaner and everything will be fine."

"No stains? What are you up to?"

"If I told you, you might write it down, and then it would be scripted."

"Right. Can't let that happen."

"Now you're catching on."

I smiled. Here we were, just two bad bros hanging out over soggy chalupas and burned fried rice. With each passing day I felt more and more comfortable around the Smear. More comfortable than I ever felt back home.

"Hello, boys," said a familiar voice.

I looked up and saw Octavia with her parents and MegaMole.

"How's the food?" asked Octavia.

The Smear smiled. *"¡Muy delicioso!"*

A waitress appeared and directed Octavia's parents and MegaMole to their table.

Before she left, Octavia leaned down and whispered in my ear, "I'm telling my parents to go home tonight. You know, less of a scene in a public place."

"Over here, dear," said Octavia's mom.

I looked over at Octavia's parents. They seemed so nice and supportive, with a super-positive vibe. Not like my parents.

Octavia caught my glance. "Embarrassing, aren't they?"

"Right," I mumbled.

"Don't forget our deal," she whispered as she walked away.

"What deal?" asked the Smear.

"Nothing," I said.

I watched Octavia sit down. While MegaMole stuffed himself with chips, Octavia leaned in with the news. There was a moment of silence, followed by a sound like a cat in a blender.

So much for not making a scene.

Octavia cried, "This is exactly why I don't want you around! You're smothering me!"

"Honey, we just want the best for you," whispered Octavia's dad.

"What's best for me right now is some space," said Octavia.

Octavia's mom managed a smile. "Sweetheart, you're too young to be on your own."

"I'll be fine. I'll be with MegaMole. What can go wrong?"

MegaMole started breathing again. Meanwhile, my appetite crawled in a little hole and died.

Octavia's dad glared at Octavia. "We're not going anywhere, young lady."

"Noooooo!" whined Octavia.

"No arguing," said Octavia's mom. "This is settled."

"You're so mean," said Octavia.

"Yes," said her dad as he led Octavia out of the restaurant. "Sometimes the good guys have to act like bad guys so they'll turn out to be better good guys."

CHAPTER 33

The Smear versus Micro-Mike battle was set to take place in an empty parking garage that allowed for multiple levels of combat. Or vacuuming. Or whatever.

As I was getting the mice ready (foot rubs, tail curls, nose buffing), the Smear walked up. "I'm not going to need them tonight," he said.

The mice were bummed.

"I got what you asked for," I said as I handed him the flyswatter and the vacuum cleaner.

"Thanks. This shouldn't take long," said the Smear as he entered the battleground.

Suddenly I got a strange feeling...

...that things were about to get strange.

It was over in about twenty seconds. In the first round! Or was it?

He lost. The Smear lost.

Wait. Maybe he was supposed to lose. I looked over to Norman.

Nope. Not supposed to lose.

I went to the Smear. "You lost!"

"I know," said the Smear.

"On purpose?"

"It sets up the rematch with MegaMole. Now I'm angry, desperate for a win. Everyone will be rooting for my comeback."

"You've done this before."

"Not my first puppet show, kid. Now excuse me while I snarl and grumble for the fans."

Okay. Messing with the script and Norman was all fun and stuff, but the problem was that the Smear was supposed to lose the rematch with MegaMole. I wanted to believe he knew what he was doing. I wanted to believe he was going to lose as planned, even though I knew he didn't want to.

Seriously, I really, *really* wanted to believe.

I just wished he wouldn't make it so hard.

CHAPTER 34

Before we started packing up, I decided to try
the black hat again. I just wanted to be prepared
in case my superpower turned out to be lasers
shooting out of my butt.

=TOOT!=

I DON'T THINK
INTERMITTENT
FARTING IS A
SUPERPOWER
EITHER

WHEW!

Norman walked up.
"Smear, I need you to come to my office."
"Why?"

"Just business," said Norman. "I need you to fill out a W7-a43 for this venue."

"I already filled out the W7-a43," said the Smear. "In triplicate."

"Well, now they want it in quadruplicate," said Norman.

"But your office smells like old socks and cheese," said the Smear.

It's true, it does.

Norman pleaded, "It'll take twenty seconds. Tops. Please?"

"I'm going to hold you to it," said the Smear. Then he turned to me. "You're coming to keep time."

"Do I have to?" I asked.

"Victor, supervillainy isn't all world domination and pie. There's paperwork. There's always paperwork."

We followed Norman to his trailer. He flung open the door, and we suddenly realized there was no paperwork. And that this meeting was going to take a lot longer than twenty seconds.

"Wow," I said. "Just like in school?"

"This isn't necessary," said the Smear.

"It is," said Smelly Feet. "You've been a bad boy."

The Smear rolled his eyes. "It's my *job* to be a bad boy!"

"But it's not your job to put the rest of us in jeopardy," said Worm Boy.

"So I've gone a little off script," said the Smear. "It's no big deal. The battles end the way they're supposed to."

"You're playing with fire. The Authority is paying attention. You don't want to be Purged, do you?" said Joe Toxic.

"And it won't be just you knitting socks in space," said Anvil Head. "We'll *all* be knitting socks in space."

"No one's going to be knitting space socks," said the Smear. "I know what I'm doing."

I wondered if that was true. I knew in my heart he wasn't a bad guy. But I wasn't sure what he knew in *his* heart. He would never risk all the supers by bringing on the Purge. I was sure of it. Pretty sure. Mostly sure. Kinda sure.

Okay, I had no idea.

"What about Dr. Deplorable?" asked Smelly Feet. "He's attacked you twice now. What did you do to get his tighty-whities in a twist?"

"Nothing," said the Smear. "He was born with his twisty-tighty-whities."

"He could come back," said Mr. Beet. "It seems like he really means business with that shark-cloud space plane."

"Not with Dave and Bob around. We'll be fine," said the Smear.

Worm Boy said, "I don't know, Dr. D. is a psychopath. His feud with Mr. Awesome ended up destroying our way of life and subjugated us all to this charade of fake posturing and phony battles."

"And guess who he blames for it all?" said Worm Boy.

"He blames me," said the Smear.

"Exactly," said Smelly Feet. "Dave and Bob can't hold him off forever. You need to fix this before it blows up in all our faces."

"Look, the life we have now isn't perfect, but it works. And we like it," said Worm Boy. "Who are you to take that away from us?" He pointed at me. "Or from him?"

The Smear looked at me. He looked sad. Not supervillain-gloomy sad. No. Heartsick sad. Sad-eyed-puppy sad.

"You're right," said the Smear. "I'm sorry. I'll do better. I'll stick to the script from now on. I'll figure out what's going on with Dr. Twisty Briefs and put a stop to it. No more funny business. Promise."

It looked convincing. It sounded convincing. And it *was* convincing. I knew it in my bones. Sure, maybe he had thought about taking down the Truce, but not now.

Not with *me* around.

CHAPTER 35

"No? What do you mean *no*?" cried Octavia.

"I can't," I said. "There's too much at stake."

It was the next day. We were back in Des Moines preparing for the big rematch with MegaMole.

Octavia cried, "There's absolutely nothing at stake! None of this means anything. It's all fake! I just want to switch places and have a little fun. You don't want me to have fun! That's it, isn't it? You're a black hole of fun. You're where fun goes to die. You work for the fun police."

I said, "Look, you don't understand. I need to
be backing the Smear tonight in case something
goes wrong."

"Wrong?"

"It's a long story."

"Start talking, Spoil."

I sighed. Then told her everything.

"Wow. That's a lot to take in," said Octavia. "I
had no idea."

I said, "It's big. And it's serious. So we can't let
anything go wrong. The Smear is scripted to lose
and that needs to happen."

Octavia slowly nodded.

"So you get it?" I asked.

"I get it. It's all perfectly clear."

"Victor, I need your help," yelled the Smear.

"I gotta go," I said to Octavia. "Wish me luck tonight."

"Good luck."

"Thanks."

"You're going to need it."

Okay. That was settled. Octavia could be a little hotheaded, but she could also be reasonable when she had to. I liked her. Not *like* like. Just regular like. She's pretty cool. Not that girls can't be cool. It's just...

I'm going to stop now.

I walked over to the Smear. He was taking inventory of the mice. He pointed to one. "Leroy here bruised his tailbone. He's sitting this battle out."

While he tended to Leroy, the Smear remarked, "You and that girl are getting tight."

"Nah," I said. "We're just friends."

"Let me give you some advice. Hero-villain relationships are difficult. You're always going to be the bad guy no matter what you do. Because, you know, you *are* the bad guy."

"She's pretty bad herself."

"She's twelve. She doesn't know what she is. Be careful with that one."

I rolled my eyes. "Sure. Careful."

"Now go get your costume on. It's almost showtime."

I went to our trailer to change. Tonight was a big night. I was excited. And nervous. It seemed like everything was going according to plan as I opened the trailer door and discovered...

CHAPTER 36

What was I supposed to do? Octavia had my costume. She was trying to be the Smear's apprentice. She couldn't be the Smear's apprentice...

I'M THE SMEAR'S APPRENTICE!

I had to stop her.

The announcer boomed, "And now the rematch you've been waiting for, the Smear versus Mega-Mole!"

"It's starting!" I cried.

I ran out to the railroad yard and yelled, "Stop!"

But it was too late. The match had already begun.

Instead of the usual posturing and insults, they got right to the action. Actually, *they* didn't. Octavia did.

I ran up to her. "Stop! Please stop!"

"Relax, dude," said Octavia. "None of this is real. I'm just having a little fun. You should try it sometime."

"You don't understand! I told you what might happen."

"Man, you're gullible. I never believed that stuff for a second. Now help me help the Smear destroy MegaMole."

"No! MegaMole has to win!" I yelled.

"No one HAS to do anything!" cried Octavia. "We get to decide!"

Dr. Deplorable was back! But this time was different. This time he made a personal appearance.

His forehead wiener dog tattoo flashed like a neon sign as he descended down a light escalator from his shark-cloud space plane.

THAT'S IT, SMEAR! YOU'RE FINISHED!

LIGHT ESCALATOR ➔

I know. Just a tad over the top.

The Smear said, "Finished?"

Dr. Deplorable aimed his elbows at the Smear. "Eliminated, erased, excised, whichever you prefer."

"Why is he pointing his elbows at us?" I asked.

The Smear whispered, "Elbow laser catapults. Very nasty."

"You again!" cried Norman, striding into the scene with his rock monsters in tow. "Are you dense? Were you dropped on your head as a baby? What part of 'You're not the authority here, I am!' don't you understand?"

"Yeah," said rock monster Bob as he shook his rock fist at Dr. D.

"What he said," added rock monster Dave, leaning in right next to him.

Last time it had been the rock monsters to the rescue. This time? Not so much.

Norman rushed up to Dr. Deplorable. "In the name of the Authority, I absolutely must insist you cease this instant. If you persist in these shenanigans, I'll have no choice but to—"

Norman never finished his wordy threat. He was too busy flying across the railroad yard while

201

contemplating his place in this particular moment in time and space.

Octavia had run away, so now it was just Dr. Deplorable, the Smear, and me.

This was a moment. A moment where you just had to go for it. No matter how silly, no matter how dangerous. You just went. NOW!

I dived at Dr. Deplorable.

I ran for cover behind the Smear.

"What are you doing?" yelled the Smear. "You could've been hurt!"

"But it worked," I said.

The Smear pointed at Dr. Deplorable. "For about fifteen seconds!"

Dr. D. turned his attention (and his elbow laser catapults) back to us. "It's over," he hissed.

He had us. There was no way out. There was only one thing standing in the way between us and oblivion: another monologue.

"Smear, you're going down!" began Dr. Deplorable. "You are the only thing standing in the way of me taking out Mr. Awesome. And now that you've shared my secret, I'm taking out your puny partner, too!"

"Seriously?" I said. "I still can't believe tickling is your secret weakness."

"A common fear brought on by a singular childhood trauma," explained Dr. Deplorable.

The Smear whispered, "His dad forgot to put the top up in the car wash and left him inside the car alone."

"Hold it," I said to Dr. Deplorable. "What about the Purge? If you destroy the Truce, what's to stop the Authority from sending us all into space, including you?"

Dr. Deplorable smiled. "With Mr. Awesome out of the way and those stone losers gone, the Authority has no muscle. There'll be nothing to stop me from TAKING OVER THE WORLD!"

"Yeah, that's another thing. You guys are always wanting to take over the world. What exactly are you going to do with it once you have it?"

"Um...I'll be in charge and everyone will have to do what I say and...and...

I stared at Dr. Deplorable. "You're insane! You'll never succeed. The entire superuniverse won't rest until you're defeated!"

The Smear glanced at me approvingly. "Nice. You're learning."

"Thanks," I said.

"ENOUGH!" boomed Dr. D. as he pointed his elbow laser catapults at us and lifted us up into the air.

Dr. Deplorable lowered us to the ground. The Smear turned to me. He looked super sad. More sad than at the peer mediation. Like if sadness were some sort of superpower. The sadness shot out of him like frowny lasers in all directions.

"What's wrong?" I asked.
Then, very softly, he said, "You."

CHAPTER 37

The Smear took a deep breath. His eyes narrowed. His face changed as he went FULL SUPERVILLAIN!

The Smear grabbed me. "You! This is all your fault! You and that stupid girl!"

"Wait. What?" I said.

"You're nothing to me now!" yelled the Smear. "You never were anything to me! I don't know why I took you on. I guess I felt sorry for you! You're the one who should be destroyed!"

He stood over me as I cowered in his massive shadow.

I whispered, "But...but...we've got each other's backs. We're...we're friends."

"You were never my friend. I just used you."

I started to cry. "No, that's not true."

"I needed you to trust me, trust me so completely that when I revealed how I really felt about you, I could finally complete my soul stain with...

...<u>YOUR</u> TEARS OF TRUE SORROW!

"It was...it was all a lie?" I whimpered.

"Of course it was a lie," said the Smear as he finished collecting my tears. "That's what I do. I'm a supervillain."

"Not for long," said Dr. Deplorable. "And I mean both of you."

The Smear turned to Dr. Deplorable. "The kid's hardly a threat. Besides, he's served his purpose. And his purpose was to provide me with THIS!" He held up the tiny vial.

"Tears of true sorrow?" asked Dr. D. "Dude, that's still seriously lame."

The Smear said, "Not when they can be used to make a superstain that can stain a man's soul and render him helpless for all eternity!"

"You know, even when we worked together back in the day, I thought the whole superstain was pretty bogus," said Dr. Deplorable.

"Don't you see? These tears will destroy Mr. Awesome," said the Smear. "He'll be left with nothing. He'll *be* nothing!"

"What about his sock-making skills?" asked Dr. Deplorable.

"Well, you never lose that," conceded the Smear.

Dr. Deplorable stared at the Smear for a few seconds. He clearly thought this was all ridiculous, but then...

"How does it work?" he asked.

The Smear said, "Two drops on his stupid

supersuit and his supersoul is stained. He instantly shrivels up into a civilian with zero superpowers. Never to be awesome again."

Dr. D. grabbed the vial from the Smear. "I don't need you. I can just soul-stain him myself."

"No, you can't. Those are just tears. You need the whole stain. I'm the only one who can make it."

"How do I know it'll work?"

"It'll work better than your elbow laser pointers. Look, I hate Awesome Boy as much as you. And besides, if I fail, you'll end me."

Dr. Deplorable smirked. "True that."

They stared at each other for a beat. Dr. D. was actually considering this.

"Okay. I'll bite," said Dr. Deplorable. "But if you're punking me, you're going to regret it. Let's blow this Popsicle stand and get to work."

My mind was reeling. None of this made any sense. Up was down. Black was white. Boxer briefs were brief boxers!

"You can't do this!" I cried. "It's not who you are. I know you. You wouldn't do this."

The Smear sneered. "You don't know me. You

never did. Now run along back to your mommy and daddy, little boy. You've served me well. I release you from your service."

Dr. Deplorable's light escalator appeared. The Smear stepped on, and the two of them (and the mice) glided up to the waiting shark-cloud space plane.

I couldn't believe what I was seeing. The Smear had betrayed me. For some stupid stain. I'd thought he cared about me. I'd thought he *liked* me. I'd thought we were *friends*. How could I have been so stupid?

I felt terrible.

I felt alone.

Absolutely alone.

No one cared about me.

Wait.

Maybe someone still did.

CHAPTER 38

"Mom? Dad? Are you there?" I said into my phone.

"Yes, Victor," said my dad. But not on the phone. His voice was coming from behind me.

I turned around to see my parents standing there. "Wait. Have you been here the whole time?"

My mom pointed to the coat around her shoulders. "Cloak of invisibility."

"It's really more of a poncho," said Dad. "We got it on sBay."

"If you were here the whole time, why didn't you do something?"

"We were respecting your need for independence," said Dad.

"Also, Dr. Deplorable is super scary," said Mom.

"It wouldn't have made any difference anyway," I said. "I was an idiot for believing in the Smear. For thinking he cared about me. Or anyone."

"We're sorry it didn't work out, son," said Dad. "We thought the Smear was the right wrong guy for you to look down to. Boy, were we wrong."

Mom put her hands out. "Here, let me give you a hug. I've been practicing."

AHHHH...

AIR HUG

"Better?" asked Mom.

"You're getting there," I said. "I'm glad you're here. I'm sorry I told you to get lost, I just…"

"You wanted to do this on your own. And you did," said Dad.

"We saw the whole thing," piped up Mom.

I nodded. "I tried my worst."

"That's all we can ask," said Dad.

I smiled (without cramping). "I appreciate the effort."

"Octavia!" yelled a woman's voice behind us.

We turned and saw Octavia's parents running toward us.

"Have you seen her?" asked Mrs. Sparkle.

Mr. Sparkle panted, "We can't find her anywhere."

"I saw her run off when Dr. Deplorable arrived," I said. "She wasn't hurt. She was grinning from ear to ear as she watched Dr. D. Wait, you don't think..."

"She would never," said Mom.

"She wouldn't dare!" added Dad.

Mr. Sparkle said, "I'm confused."

I wasn't. Octavia had taken off with Dr. Deplorable and the Smear. That was what she'd wanted all along. To become a supervillain's apprentice.

CHAPTER 39

"NOOOOOO!" cried Octavia's mom.

"She would never do that!" said Mr. Sparkle. "She's a *good* girl!"

I said. "Octavia? This is your daughter we're talking about, right?"

"She just has issues. You know, acting out. Being contrary," said Mrs. Sparkle.

OH, YEAH, BEEN THERE, BIRTHED THAT.

I rolled my eyes. If I'd learned one thing over the last few days, it was that good and bad were meaningless and superficial. The Smear had seemed good but turned out bad. Dr. Deplorable had seemed bad but turned out worse. And Octavia? She wasn't bad. She was just bored.

And now she was in danger.

I said, "She must have slipped up Dr. Deplorable's light escalator when no one was looking."

"That was one sweet light escalator," said my dad.

"Can you just order that online?" asked Mr. Sparkle.

Dad said, "No. That looks like custom work to me."

"Hello!" I yelled. "We're getting off topic!"

"What is the topic again?" asked Mom.

I sighed. "Octavia? Dr. Deplorable and the Smear's evil plot to bring down Mr. Awesome and the Authority and take over the world?"

"Oh, right," said Mom.

Silence. Finally.

"We should call the Authority," said Mr. Sparkle.

I shook my head. "No. Without the rock mon-sters, the Authority is just Norman shaking his finger and frowning a lot."

"Okay," said Mrs. Sparkle. "What do we do?"

I said, "We all work together to find Octavia and stop Dr. Deplorable and the Smear!"

"We can't work together," said Mom.

"We're mortal enemies. No offense," said Mrs. Sparkle.

Mom said, "None taken."

"You're FAKE mortal enemies!" I screamed. "It's not real! None of this is real! Except for Octavia getting hurt and Dr. D. taking over the world! That part is VERY, VERY real!"

More silence. Then...

"Can we take separate space planes?" asked Mrs. Sparkle.

"Sure," I said.

"Will we have to share meals?" asked my mom.

Mrs. Sparkle cried, "What's that supposed to mean?"

"It's just that Mr. Spoil here is on a low-carb diet, and I know how you people like your sweets. You know, goody-goody, sugar and spice, nothing naughty, everything nice."

"That's a filthy stereotype!" said Mrs. Sparkle. "Sure, we like the occasional tiramisu, though it can make Mr. Sparkle gassy."

What is it with superadults? I swear they age backward. They start out wise and slowly lose the ability to tie their shoes.

I said, "Okay, are we good now? Everyone on the same page about rescuing Octavia and saving our superfuture?"

Everyone nodded.

"Where do we start?" asked Mr. Sparkle.

"The Smear's secret lair," I said. "They can't go after Mr. Awesome until he creates the superstain."

Mrs. Sparkle said, "We should warn Mr. Awesome."

Octavia's mom took out her cell phone, put it on speaker, and dialed.

"Press one for English, two for Spanish," chirped the phone.

Mrs. Sparkle pressed one.

"Listen carefully to the prompts, as our menu has changed," said the phone. "Press one for emergency earthquakes, tsunamis, and alien invasions. Press two for evil-lair extermination. Press three for supermarket openings and school visits. Press four for the end of the world. Press five for a signed photo. Press six to hear this menu again. Press zero to talk to a customer service representative."

Mrs. Sparkle pressed zero.

"We appreciate your call. All of our operators are busy with other customers. Your wait time is approximately...

And they let these people operate space planes.

CHAPTER 40

"So *this* is the Smear's secret lair?" said my dad.

THE WILLOWS OF FORESTBROOK

"Nothing says secret lair like the Willows of Forestbrook," said Mom.

"Which apartment is it?" asked Mr. Sparkle.
My mom pointed. "I'm thinking that one."

"What's the plan?" I asked.
"Just follow me," said Mrs. Sparkle as she took
the scenic route to the apartment.

THE
WILLOWS
OF
FORESTBROOK

"Or we could take the stairs," said my mom.

With that, the rest of us sensibly climbed the stairs and gathered in front of the Smear's door. Some of us were a bit more winded than others.

"Who's going to break down the door?" asked Mr. Sparkle.

"I would, but I just had shoulder surgery," said my dad.

"If only we had Anvil Head," said Mom. "He's really handy in these situations."

"But then he just hangs around with nothing to do," said Mrs. Sparkle.

"We could knock," I offered.

"Knock? Supervillains don't knock," said Mom.

"Which is why you villains have no respect for privacy," said Mrs. Sparkle.

"Privacy is for wimps!" cried Dad.

"I'm knocking," I said.

I knocked. The door moved. I pushed it open to reveal the aftermath of a smear-stained Armageddon. It looked like a dragon had barfed after eating a bad knight.

"Octavia!" called Mrs. Sparkle.

"I'll check the bedroom and the closets," said Mom.

"WAIT!" I shouted. "It could be booby-trapped!"

Everyone took a step back.

Mrs. Sparkle pointed to Mr. Sparkle's elbow. "Those stains never wash out."

"I need something to roll into the room, see if it trips anything," I said.

Mom reached into her cloak. "How about this?"

"What?" she said. "You never know when you'll need a bowling ball."

Mr. Sparkle pointed inside the apartment. "Wait. Look!"

A stain-splattered cat sat staring at us. Without incident.

"I think we'll be fine," said Mr. Sparkle.

We all stepped into the apartment and began to search. There was nothing. No Smear. No Octavia and no superstain.

"Where did they go?" asked Mrs. Sparkle.

I hadn't a clue until I looked up.

"It's the Bostocalypse all over again," said Dad. "They destroyed the city once. Now they're going to destroy it again. And destroy all the supers in the process."

"We're doomed!" cried Mom.

I sprinted out of the apartment. "Not if we hurry."

CHAPTER 41

After convincing the Sparkles that ride sharing was both environmentally correct and, more importantly, cheaper, we all boarded Anvil Head's space plane and headed to Boston.

We were somewhere over Ohio, hitting Mach 8, when Mrs. Sparkle asked, "How are we going to find Octavia in a big city like Boston?"

Good question. She *could* be anywhere, with or without the Smear and Dr. Deplorable. But I had an idea.

I took out my phone and started searching. "We know the battle will be at that big park in the middle of the city."

"Boston Common," said Dad.

"Right," I continued. "So it's logical to assume they're staying somewhere nearby. Ah, here it is."

Mr. Sparkle said, "What makes you think we'll find them there?"

"Free self-serve breakfast. The Smear loves to make his own waffles."

"Yeah, Phil really likes his waffles," said my dad.

"Who's Phil?" I said.

"The Smear," said Dad. "His real name is Phil. Phil Huluwitski."

"I didn't know that Phil was the Smear," said Mom. "Why didn't I recognize him?"

"It's the mask. And, you know, the weight gain," said Dad.

"You knew the Smear?" I asked.

Dad said, "We grew up with him. Down the street. Who were his parents again?"

"The Malevolent Horde. Ray and Liz," said Mom.

"Ah, that's right. You wouldn't think two could make a horde, but Ray and Liz made it work," said Dad.

"Phil was a strange child," said Mom. "So polite and helpful. Used to drive his parents nuts. Kind of like...

Wait. Phil was like me? No, it couldn't be. The Smear was a treacherous liar who'd betrayed my trust (*and* stolen my tears). He was nothing like me!

"That means there's hope for Victor," said Mom.

Dad said, "How so?"

"Well, Phil was a good kid who grew up to be the evil Smear. Sure, he had a rocky start, but now look at him! He's on his way to take down Mr. Awesome and take over the world."

"Hey, you're right," said Dad, nodding.

"No, you're not right," I said. "We've been over this. The Smear and Dr. Deplorable are putting all of us at risk of being Purged with their stupid takedown of Mr. Awesome. It doesn't matter if he was a good or bad kid. All that matters is what he's doing right now!"

"Oh, right," said Mom. "I keep forgetting."

"You have to admit the good-bad/bad-good thing is a bit confusing," added Dad. "And unsettling. I mean, look at us cooperating and sharing a ride with you know who."

"Superheroes," Mom whispered.

WE'RE SITTING RIGHT HERE.

Mom smiled. "No offense."

Mrs. Sparkle smiled. "Tons taken."

This whole plan was doomed. What was I thinking, trying to team up heroes and villains to do something positive, something proactive, something *useful*? I wasn't good. Or bad. I was nuts!

I answered, "Hello?"

A very familiar voice on the other end said, "Hey, um, Victor? Hey, it's me, Octavia. I...um...

CHAPTER 42

"You're not supposed to be using a cell phone on a plane. It messes with the electronics," said Mrs. Sparkle.

"That's a myth," said my dad. "They tell you that so you won't spend all your time on the phone instead of paying $9.99 to watch the in-flight movie: *Fatman Versus Überman*."

FATMAN vs. ÜBERMAN

GUT IMPLANTS ↓

THIGH IMPLANTS ←

"What a stupid premise," said my mom. "I mean, seriously, Überman is made of carbon fiber and hate, and Fatman is made of, you know, fat."

"QUIET!" I yelled. Then back to the phone. "Octavia, is that you?"

"Octavia!" screamed Mrs. Sparkle. "My baby!"

Octavia said, "Tell my mother I'm not a baby."

I turned to Mrs. Sparkle. "She says she's not a baby."

"Okay, dear," said Mrs. Sparkle. "You're a confused tween who's in completely over her head."

"Let's stick with baby," said Octavia.

"Where are you? We're coming to get you," I said.

"I don't know," she said. "They blindfolded me. All I can tell you is it smells like waffles."

I smiled. "I know exactly where you are."

"I'm scared," said Octavia.

"I know," I said. "We'll be there soon."

She whispered, "Someone's coming. Gotta go."

And she hung up.

"Is she okay? Where is she? Why didn't she want to talk to us?" asked Mrs. Sparkle.

I said, "She had to go. She's fine. She's exactly where I thought she would be."

"Where did she get a phone?" said my dad.

"Super question," I said.

Mom said, "Maybe they let her call us so we'd come and they could ambush us."

"Or," said Mr. Sparkle, "they forced Octavia to make the call and put a trace on the phone to find out exactly where we are."

"Someone's firing at us!" I yelled.

I rushed to the cockpit to see Dr. Deplorable's shark-cloud space plane blasting lasers our way.

Anvil Head took evasive action, but the laser fire was relentless.

Anvil Head shouted, "The shields! They can't take much more!"

"We're going down," I said softly.

"What?" yelled Mrs. Sparkle.

I screamed, "We're going down!"

"No! That is completely unacceptable," she said. "Out of my way. I'm taking over the controls!"

Mrs. Sparkle pushed past me to the cockpit. "This is my plane now," she barked. "Watch and learn."

Anvil Head let go of the stick, and Mrs. Sparkle took a seat and put the space plane into a steep dive.

Mrs. Sparkle said, "We have to fly low, where they'll be forced to think about collateral damage."

"You can't use civilians for cover," said Mr. Sparkle.

My mom rolled her eyes. "Superheroes and their rules."

"No worries," said Mrs. Sparkle. "Where we're going, there are no civilians."

We were flying at treetop level now over a heavily wooded area. No towns. No roads. No civilians. Any second now Dr. Deplorable was going to realize he could fire at will.

"Where is it? Where is it? Bingo! There it is," cried Mrs. Sparkle.

I pointed. "Um, that's a waterfall. And we're headed straight toward it."

Mrs. Sparkle nodded. "Uh-huh. Now be a good dear and brace for impact."

We were alive. But I couldn't see a thing. "Where are we?" I asked.

CHAPTER 43

"I didn't know heroes had secret lairs," said Mom.

Mr. Sparkle said, "If you knew, then it wouldn't be a secret lair, would it?"

"It's just I always thought your type masqueraded as civilians," said Mom. "You know, reporters, billionaires, Norse gods, golf pros."

"Don't believe everything you read," said Mrs. Sparkle. "But you're right about the golf pros."

"I knew it," said Mom.

As secret lairs went, it was pretty cool. It checked off all your basic secret-lair furnishings. There were stacks of ammunition (sparklers), spare costumes, a lot of really old blinking and buzzing computers, a doomsday clock (no secret lair is complete without a doomsday clock), and a surprisingly not-too-lame Sparklemobile.

Something's missing," said my mom.

"No minions," said Dad.

Mr. Sparkle sighed. "We call them superspecial helpers."

Dad said, "That could explain why they're all gone."

"We had to lay them off after the Truce," said Mrs. Sparkle. "Poor dears. A lot of them ended up in day care. I don't know why."

"Now what?" I said. "We're still not in Boston."

"Aerial robot recon," said Mrs. Sparkle as she went over to a computer monitor and started typing.

After a few seconds an invisible door slid open and a flying blender emerged.

It started to rap. "Whip is my name. Betta than James. I got me some game. So don't be all lame. When you shower me with fame."

"We got it on sBay," explained Mrs. Sparkle. "It has three vocal settings: hip-hop, middle school vice principal, and heartless British villain."

"Not a lot of good choices there," I remarked.

Mrs. Sparkle continued poking at the keyboard. "Since they now know we're coming, we're going to need Whip to fly into Boston, scope out the terrain, and put eyes on Octavia."

"How long is that going to take?" I asked.

Dad asked, "Where's the little villains' room?"

"Down the hall, right past the Wall of Shame," said Mr. Sparkle.

Mrs. Sparkle said, "So, Victor, you're sure they're at the Vacation Inn Express?"

"Follow the waffles," I said.

"Gotcha. We now have live video from Boston Common," said Mrs. Sparkle.

We watched on the monitor as Whip entered a hotel.

"There he is!" I shouted.

Mrs. Sparkle punched at the keyboard, and Whip responded by ducking down under a chair. Meanwhile, the Smear gave up with the desk clerk and headed toward the elevator. Whip followed at a safe distance. We watched the Smear get into the elevator. As the doors closed, Whip tilted up. The elevator stopped at the fourth floor.

"How's Whip going to get up there?" I asked.

"The stairs?" said Mr. Sparkle.

Whip moved to the stairwell. But there was a door blocking his way.

I said, "Now what—"

I nodded. "That works."

Whip zoomed up the stairs and blasted through the door to the fourth floor. He turned down the hall just as a door was closing.

"Octavia has to be in there," said Mr. Sparkle.

"We'll find out in a second," said Mrs. Sparkle.

Whip flew down the hall to where the door had

closed. He tilted up. There was an air-condition-
ing vent.

Whip blasted through the vent and into the
air duct. He flew slowly, looking for a vent to the
room.

SLAM! BAM! CRASH!

"Oops, upside down," said Mrs. Sparkle as she
flipped the image.

"There she is!" cried Mr. and Mrs. Sparkle.

"She's not tied up," I said.

"She doesn't look like a hostage," said Mom.

"She looks...um...

CHAPTER 44

We arrived at the hotel in the Sparklemobile. We covered up the detailing so we'd be more inconspicuous.

We staked out the hotel and waited. In the meantime, the parents argued.

After what seemed (and was) hours, we finally saw the Smear and Dr. Deplorable exit the hotel.

"There they are!" said Mom.

"They're certainly chummy," noted Mrs. Sparkle.

They weren't just chummy—they were pals, besties, *friends!*

Stupid superjerks.

We watched them walk down the street and enter a Starbucks. I knew they'd be in there a while, because coffee makes the Smear go and he likes a clean restroom.

"Okay, let's go," said Dad. "I'll be the lookout while the rest of you go get Octavia."

Mrs. Sparkle's eyes narrowed. "How can we trust you?"

"Hello, you'll have my son," said Dad.

I gave Mrs. Sparkle a little wave.

Mrs. Sparkle said, "So you hold us hostage and we hold you hostage."

"Right. It's called trust," said Mom.

"Trust *you?*" said Mr. Sparkle.

"Look, you and us, we're not that different," said Dad. "Sure, we're villains. We like to conquer, enslave, and destroy. You're heroes. You like to serve, protect, and give your reconobot a stupid name. But at the end of the day we're just two sides of the same—"

"Coin," I said.

"Right," said Dad. "A coin that's made of loyalty, trust, and super-high-quality butt-kicking."

"I get it," said Mrs. Sparkle. "We're heads and you're tails."

"No," said Mom. "We're heads and you're tails."

I'd had enough. While the parents bickered, I slipped out of the van and ran into the hotel. I entered the elevator and punched the button for the fourth floor. The doors opened, and I turned and walked down the hall. I stopped in front of Octavia's room and...

"Octavia, are you okay?" I asked.

"Of course. Why wouldn't I be?" she said.

I raised my eyebrows. "Gee, you're hanging out with two world-destroying superlosers and you just arranged an attack on your own parents."

"What?"

"Your phone call. It was traced to our space plane. Dr. Deplorable sent one of his goons to shoot us down."

Octavia was incredulous. "You're lying."

"I'm not. We had to ditch in your parents' secret lair."

"Joe and Phil would never do that. We're teammates. They need me."

"I see you're on a first-name basis."

"They're *good* bad guys. I'm like them. They're like me. I can't help that I was born to good parents. For once in my life I feel like I belong. No. You're not going to take that away from me with your lies. That phone call was just a joke."

"They're using you, Octavia. They're using you to lure us in and get rid of us so they can superstain Mr. Awesome, break the Truce, destroy the Authority, and take over the world!"

"It's not true!" yelled Octavia.

"It *is* true," said a voice behind us.

We spun around.

CHAPTER 45

"It can't be!" said Octavia.

"Of course it is," laughed the Smear. "You were just a means to an end. You don't think we actually needed you."

Octavia screamed, "You tried to kill my parents?"

"Yes. Unfortunately, I missed," said the Smear.

"You were at the controls?" I said.

The Smear shook his head. "When are you going to learn, Victor? I am not your friend."

I couldn't speak. How could I have been so wrong about him?

The Smear chuckled, "And now I'm going to take care of both of you...once and for all."

"Not so fast," said a familiar voice at the door.

It was Mom, along with the Sparkles.

"Mom! Dad!" cried Octavia happily.

"Where's Dad?" I said.

"He's on lookout," said Mom.

Mrs. Sparkle pointed to the Smear. "And a fine job he's doing."

I said, "He obviously slipped by while you were arguing."

"Heads," growled Mrs. Sparkle.

"Tails," Mom growled back.

The Smear looked at Octavia and me. "Wow. It all makes sense now. You can't help who you are with parents like these. You were doomed from the start."

Mrs. Sparkle yelled, "Whip! Attack!"

Nothing happened. Everyone looked at one another.

"Whip?"

Still nothing. Then...

"What the...?" said the Smear.

"ATTACK!" screamed Mrs. Sparkle.

Whip attacked. The Smear defended himself. And then things got messy.

They backed the Smear onto the balcony. There was nowhere for him to turn when he hopped up on the railing.

"You're not going to stop us!" cried the Smear. "You're too…

Octavia and I ran to the railing. There was nothing and no one on the ground below.

"Where'd he go?" I shouted.

Octavia cried, "I don't see him!"

"What *is* that?" I said.

Octavia said, "It's coming from the Common."

I looked at my parents.

They both nodded.

Then I knew. It was Mr. Awesome and Dr. Deplorable.

The battle had begun.

CHAPTER **46**

Let's recap. Dr. Deplorable was on Boston Common to battle Mr. Awesome. The Smear had disappeared over the railing with the superstain on his way to Dr. D. The Sparkles were reunited with Octavia (but had a few questions about why she seemed to have helped try to shoot them out of the sky). Dad and Mom were monologuing. Again.

WHO JUST OWNED THE SMEAR? WE DID! WITH SUPERIOR KICK-BUTTERY! YEAH! THAT'S A WORD! I JUST MADE IT UP!

OH, LORD...

THAT'S WHAT WE DO! KICK BUTT AND MAKE UP WORDS!

"We have to get to the Common to stop the Smear!" I cried.

"Wait," said Octavia as she turned to her parents. "Mom, Dad...I'm sorry. I didn't know they were tracing the call. I thought they needed me. I thought they wanted me."

"We want you," said Mrs. Sparkle.

Mr. Sparkle added, "No matter what."

I KNOW THAT NOW!

"Oh, so that's how you do it," said Mom.

"We need to go NOW!" I insisted.

"Yes," said Mr. Sparkle. "What's the plan?"

I'd had it with these bozos. No more Mr. Nice Supervillain.

STOP THE SMEAR
FROM HELPING DR.
DEPLORABLE TAKE
OVER THE WORLD BY
DESTROYING MR.
AWESOME!

Mom's eyes popped. "Now *that's* my bossy boy!"

"I think I'm going to cry," said Dad.

Octavia was at the door. "Are we going or not?"

"We're going!" I growled.

Finally we went. Out of the hotel. And straight to the Common. When we arrived, I set up a surveillance plan to find the Smear.

"The parents will circle the perimeter of the crowd for the Smear, while Octavia and I look from the front," I said. "If you see him, don't confront him. Call me. And we'll call you if we see him. It'll take all of us to stop him from using the superstain."

My dad walked up holding my black hat. "You left this in the van. Put it on. You never know when your superpower will kick in."

"Dad," I said. "It's not going to help. I don't think I'm ever going to get superpowers or that I even want them anymore."

Mom said, "Superpowers, good and bad, are a gift. Put the hat on."

She said it in that supervillain-mom you're-in-big-trouble-if-you-don't-do-what-I-tell-you voice. I put the hat on.

Everyone went about their tasks while Octavia and I pushed into the crowd.

"Our top priority is to keep the Smear from getting his superstain to Dr. Deplorable," I said.

Octavia said, "How exactly are we going to do that?"

I shook my head. "I have no idea."

We got to the front.

"That sound again," said Octavia.

"Mr. Awesome...," I said.

"...and his Sonic Staff."

Octavia let out a breath. "Whoa."

Yeah, *whoa*. The biggest supers were battling for the fate of the world.

And *we* had to stop them.

No biggie.

I scanned the crowd. No trace of the Smear. I looked back to the battle. The fans were really into it. They had no idea Dr. Deplorable was making it a real-life battle. But I knew what was up. And Mr. Awesome was figuring it out too.

Nearby I spotted the referees, the Pollinator and Lasso Girl.

I was just about to get their attention when the Pollinator dropped his water bottle and bent over to get it.

I would recognize that underwear anywhere.

"That's not the Pollinator," I yelled. "That's…

CHAPTER 47

Okay, you know how time slows down during an emergency? Stuff that takes seconds seems to take hours? Well, this wasn't like that. What happened next went fast. *Super* fast. I can barely remember the details. But I can tell you exactly how I felt.

I felt scared.

No, *terrified*. Like lying wide awake when I was six, waiting for the monsters underneath my bed to eat me.

In the past I would have followed the rules for dealing with monsters, which was to put on my bike helmet and hide in the closet.

But now there were no rules. I had to figure it out for myself. And it was obvious what I had to do.

"I'm going after him," I said.

Octavia grabbed me. "No. Call our parents. You can't stop him alone!"

I pointed. "Look! He's already heading toward Dr. Deplorable. There's no time!"

"No, Victor!" cried Octavia.

I shook her off and took off after the Smear. As far as the fans knew, I was part of the act. Nobody stopped me as I sprinted toward the battle.

As I grew closer, I saw he was holding the vials of superstain. He was about to hand them to Dr. Deplorable. I had to do something before he destroyed Mr. Awesome, the Truce, and...*the world*.

No pressure.

I jumped high and hard.

SUPER TICKLING!

    I had Dr. D. down. I really did. He was completely at my mercy. I was just about to finish him off when...

275

The Smear slimed me with a sticky-goo bomb.
I was mired in muck, covered in ooze. I struggled,
but it was no use. I wasn't going anywhere.

It was over.

Except for the monologue.

"Okay, I got it!" I yelled. "You're the big bad guy. Good for you. I have just one question."

The Smear stared at me.

"Why?" I asked.

While Dr. Deplorable and Mr. Awesome traded blasts behind us, the Smear told me...

Wait. What? Pretend? He was pretending? When? Before...or now?

The Smear started to walk away.

"STOP!" I yelled.

The Smear didn't stop. He was determined to help Dr. Deplorable destroy Mr. Awesome once and for all.

I struggled to free myself from my sticky-goo prison, but it was useless. It was all about to be over. And I had a front-row seat.

A front-row seat to watch it all end.

CHAPTER 48

I watched helplessly as the Smear and Dr. Deplorable stood over the sticky-gooed Mr. Awesome.

The Common was scorched. The crowd was gone, having scattered in all directions the second they realized the fake battle had suddenly become very, *very* real. And very, very dangerous.

"This wasn't in the script," remarked Mr. Awesome from inside his sticky-goo prison.

Dr. Deplorable smiled. "From here on out there won't be any more scripts. No more play-acting. All battles will be real. All outcomes *final*."

"You're breaking the Truce," said Mr. Awesome.

"We're *nuking* the Truce," said Dr. D.

"What about the Authority and the Purge?"

"They'll cease to exist, thanks to our secret weapon," said Dr. Deplorable. "Show him,
Smear."

The Smear produced two vials. "One is the
base of tears of true sorrow," he said. "And the
other is the soul stain activator."

"A superstain that can stain a man's soul?" said
Mr. Awesome. "That is seriously lame."

"No. It's my ticket to world domination," said
Dr. Deplorable.

Mr. Awesome scoffed. "I don't believe you.
How do I know it works?"

Dr. Deplorable smiled. "We're about to find out. Smear, hand me the vials, please."

The Smear stepped toward Dr. Deplorable. He had a strange look in his eyes. And he was smiling. Then, just as he raised the two vials, I heard a voice scream...

NOOOOOOO!

Dr. Deplorable raised the two superstain vials above his head with one hand, while Octavia squirmed in the other.

Dr. Deplorable said, "Before we take out Mr. Awesome, we should test it first on Sparkle Junior here. I mean, we wouldn't want to waste Mr. Awesome's time with a malfunctioning soul stain...

The Smear put his hands up. "Trust me, it works. You don't have to test it."

"Trust you? The man who branded my forehead with a wiener dog?" said Dr. Deplorable. "I think not. Now hold still, sweetie."

"NO!" I screamed from my sticky-goo trap. "Let her go. Test it on me!"

"What difference does it make?" asked Dr. Deplorable.

"She has no soul!" I yelled. "I do!"

Octavia said, "Hey!"

"That was mean," said Dr. D. "Although you

did try to kill your parents, so he sort of has a point."

"You set me up!" cried Octavia.

"But you enjoyed it. I could tell," said Dr. Deplorable.

Dr. D. let Octavia go. "Release the boy and let's get this over with," he said to the Smear.

Octavia ran to her parents. Meanwhile, Mom and Dad rushed the Smear. He stood in front of me and pointed his Stain Blaster at my parents.

"No!" I shouted.

The Smear yanked me out of the goo and smiled. "Let's go stain a soul, shall we?"

"NO!" I screamed. "Let's not!"

He threw me over his shoulder and carried me toward Dr. Deplorable.

"Put me down!" I screamed.

But he didn't seem to hear me. I twisted my head to look up. It was like he was in a trance, with his eyes narrowed and his lips twisted into a cruel, stain-eating grin.

"Mr. Smear, please!" I begged. "This isn't who you are! You said you needed me. You said we were in this together. Always! Remember? *Remember?*"

But he didn't answer. I looked back at my parents, flailing in the sticky goo. They couldn't help me. I turned to find Octavia struggling as her parents held her back.

"Victor, no!" she yelled.

"It's okay," I said to Octavia. "I'll be okay."

We approached Dr. Deplorable and stopped. He stood with one foot on Mr. Awesome's neck.

"Wait," said the Smear. "Let me do it."

"What?" I cried.

The Smear pointed to Dr. Deplorable's tattoo. "After what I did to you, I have to prove my loyalty. What better way than to destroy my former apprentice?"

"You really are evil!" I yelled.

Dr. Deplorable smiled. "I've always had my doubts, but when he opened fire on your plane, I knew he had the wrong stuff. Supervillains can smell these things, and the Smear here smells like fire and weasels and putrid rotting eggplant with just a hint of nutmeg."

The Smear grinned back. "Just a hint."

Dr. Deplorable handed the two vials to the Smear.

As the Smear took the soul stain, I could feel my whole body start to shake. "No! Please, no!"

The Smear poured the stain activator into the tears of true sorrow, then he turned to me. "This will all be over soon."

"How can you do this?" I said.

"Easy. Once you figure out who you really are, deep down, then you have the power to do exactly what needs to be done."

"I don't understand."

"You will. Someday soon, you will."

"Please don't," I pleaded.

The Smear smiled. "I have to. I don't have a choice."

"You always have a choice," I said.

"Not this time."

One last-ditch effort to save my soul…

I looked him in the eyes. "This isn't you."

The Smear winked. "You're right…"

BUBBLE-BUBBLE *HISSSS*

The Smear and I stood over what was left of Dr. Deplorable.

I said, "You stopped pretending."

The Smear smiled. "And did my job."

CHAPTER 49

"You were trying to take Dr. Deplorable down the whole time?" I asked.

"Not the whole time," said the Smear. "In the beginning, when we first met, I was just trying to make a comeback. But once Dr. D. showed up, I knew he would never let that happen, because I'm the only one who knows his weakness."

"Tickling. His weakness turned out to be my superpower?"

"Who knew?"

"Whoa!" It was still hard to believe.

"Once he monologued his plan, I had no choice but to turn on you so he would leave you alone."

"In order to save me."

The Smear smiled. "In order to save everybody!"

"But wait," I said. "I still have one question."

"Always with the questions."

"Why save anybody? You're a supervillain. You could have gone along with Dr. D. and taken over the world. That would have been the ultimate comeback!"

"It was you."

"Me?"

YOU SAID I WAS AWESOME. AWESOME PEOPLE DON'T TAKE OVER THE WORLD. BECAUSE, THEY DON'T NEED TO, BECAUSE YOU KNOW. THEY'RE AWESOME!

"It's true," said Mr. Awesome, who was eavesdropping.

"So I'm the Tickler," I said.

"Yeah, I know it's weird," said the Smear. "You can pick your nose, but you can't pick your superpower."

"That's gross."

The Smear shrugged. "I'm a supervillain."

"Me too!" I said.

The Smear smiled. "You too."

Octavia ran up to the Smear. She wasn't happy. "Hey, you used me to get the coordinates on the plane!"

"If I had wanted to shoot the plane down, I would've shot the plane down," said the Smear. "It was just to stay in Dr. Deplorable's good graces."

Mr. Awesome stuck his hand out to the Smear. "I suppose a thank-you is in order."

The Smear shook his hand. "Just doing my job."

"Pretending to be a supervillain," said Mr. Awesome.

"No, not pretending. I acted to save the people I care about. Rest assured I still hate you with every fiber of my being," said the Smear. "I just don't hate myself anymore. Victor here helped me see it takes a hero to make a villain."

I smiled.

The Smear put his hand over his mouth. "Did I just say that out loud?"

"You *are* a hero," I said.

"Language!" cried the Smear. "You kiss your mom with that mouth?"

"Not until now," said my mom, dripping with sticky goo. She came up to me, put her arms out, and gave me a real hug. With touching and everything! Then—gasp!—she kissed my forehead.

"That felt weird," said Mom.

"That felt good," I said.

Meanwhile, Dr. Deplorable was coming to.

"What happened?" asked Dr. Deplorable. "Where am I?"

"Is he still a threat?" I asked.

"Not anymore," said the Smear.

Mr. Awesome approached Octavia and me. "I think you two have a very bright future in the superworld. I can pull a few strings. How would you like to move up in the ranks?"

Octavia and I looked at each other. Then looked at our parents.

"Do I have to be a hero?" asked Octavia.

Her parents winced.

"Do I have to be a villain?" I asked.

My parents sighed.

"Whatever you want," said Mr. Awesome.

I looked at the Smear and smiled.

EPILOGUE

In the end Octavia and I decided to stay in our respective supercorners. I'm now...

Yeah, it's lame until I get you on those sensitive spots on your sides just below your rib cage.

It's torture! Well, not real torture. Fun torture. If you think about it, it's the perfect superpower for me. I can lay you out, but I can't really hurt you, and you'll be laughing the whole time. I can be bad but still be good. You know, in a bad way that's actually good.

Sort of. I think. Let's move on.

As for Octavia, she got her superpower a few weeks later (which I tease her about constantly). Are you ready for this? Seriously, she's now...

C'mon, she's a Sparkle...you knew it was going to be something artsy-craftsy.

At first she was pretty upset. But once she got a handle on the nuisance properties of glitter, she got on board fast.

Octavia and I now battle on the Junior Super Circuit against other beginner supervillains and superheroes. Some of the battles can get a little unstructured.

But it's fun and that's the point. With Dr. Deplorable out of the way, the superbattles are no longer winner takes all, but winner picks up the root beers after the battle.

My parents are back to semiretirement and trying to cope with their new affection skills.

Octavia's parents are as obnoxiously positive as ever.

Mr. Awesome has returned to opening shopping malls and grocery stores.

And Dr. Deplorable? Well, he's gone. The Smear wasn't too clear about what happens when your soul gets stained. Let's just say world domination is the last thing on his mind.

Meanwhile, the Smear is hard at work writing his memoirs.

He stays in touch. He still takes time to show me some pointers. He's always reminding me what's really important.

ABOUT THE AUTHOR

MICHAEL FRY has been a cartoonist for over thirty years and is the co-creator and writer of the *Over the Hedge* comic strip, which was turned into a DreamWorks film starring Bruce Willis and William Shatner. He lives near Austin, Texas.